THE GREATEST SURVIVOR STORIES NEVER TOLD

Mara Bovsun and Allan Zullo

**Andrews McMeel
Publishing**

Kansas City

02 03 04 05 06 VAI 10 9 8 7 6 5 4 3 2 1

ISBN: 0-7407-2728-1

Library of Congress Control Number: 2002103636

To Michael

—M.B.

To my wife, Kathy,
who has survived more than
35 years of marriage.

—A.Z.

Acknowledgments

Many thanks to David Smith of the New York Public Library for his excellent ideas and guidance through the collection, and to Jay Maeder, Danny Burstein, and Selma Bovsun for their wonderful suggestions and support.

Contents

Introduction:

NEVER
SAY
DIE

Contestants in the hit TV series *Survivor* go through a lot in their quest for big money. They endure muscle-numbing tests, run through peculiar obstacle courses, and eat disgusting bugs. They drop pounds, grow beards, get sunburned, look grubby, and turn cranky. It's called reality television.

Yeah, right. Compared to the true survivor stories in this book, what contestants go through on *Survivor* is a Sunday picnic on a manicured lawn.

On *Survivor,* a wrong move means you're voted off the island. In the real world of survival, a wrong move means you're dead. On *Survivor,* the prize for doing everything right is a million bucks. In the real world of survival, the prize for doing everything right is your very life.

Psychologists say that each of us humans has an inherent survival instinct that lies dormant—in fact, that is virtually unknown to us—and doesn't emerge until we are battling toe-to-toe with death. Only then does that instinct reveal itself and come to our aid to combat any or all of the six basic enemies of survival: thirst, cold, hunger, pain, terror, and loneliness.

"It's the human spirit recognizing that someday you will die but, by God, you will do whatever you need to do to hold it off today," says Charles Figley, a psychologist at Florida State University.

Whether you're a highly trained member of a SWAT team or an elementary school teacher, you possess that survival instinct. That's why the survivors in this book represent all walks of life: a New York millionaire businessman, a teenage Cuban stowaway, and a Pennsylvania coal miner are among them. And their life-and-death encounters occurred all over the globe: the barren, sun-baked Arizona desert; the frozen, snow-whipped Canadian wasteland; the steamy, deadly Amazon jungle.

Despite overwhelming odds, you can survive the seemingly most hopeless predicament if you're willing to do the unthinkable. As you'll read in this book, desperation knows no limits. A prospector who is lost in the desert for nearly a week without water drinks his own urine to survive. A teenager with her arms hacked off staggers for over three miles to get help.

Introduction

Real-life struggles are often solitary encounters. Survivors must face their fate alone—being imprisoned in a dark hole, lost in a mountain wilderness, or abandoned for years on a deserted island—with no one to comfort or advise them, no voice of authority telling them what to do next.

And even if you are among thousands suffering, you alone must bear your own pain. During the horrific terrorist attacks on the World Trade Center, it was "walk or die" for an NYPD chief police surgeon who was suffering painful, potentially fatal internal bleeding after being struck by falling debris. An NYPD lieutenant was badly injured in the collapse of the South Tower of the World Trade Center; she staggered out of the rubble only to be seriously hurt again when the North Tower gave way.

In most cases, we never know when that survival instinct will kick in because the specter of death usually appears so unexpectedly. A plane explodes in midair. A building blows up. A hotel fire breaks out. These and other calamities described in this book proved fatal for thousands of victims. And yet, as you'll see, these tragedies produced amazing stories of survival. The survivors' accounts aren't well known; many have been long forgotten; others received only local media coverage.

Who are these survivors? What's special about them? It would be easy to imagine that they are somehow smarter, stronger, or younger than the rest of us, but that's certainly not the case.

The survivors called on their survival instinct to overcome their fears and keep their wits about them in the face of a horror that might have paralyzed others. "Fear defeats more people than any other one thing in the world," said Ralph Waldo Emerson. Survivors in this book felt the terror; they just weren't consumed by it.

Experts have no formula for who's going to survive a life-and-death situation. Some people pray; others curse. Some stay calm and think things through; others react impulsively and take bold actions.

If there is one common thread among survivors, it's a refusal to give in to death without a fight—a willingness to keep trying something, anything, to live. It might mean crawling for days in the wilderness with two fractured ankles or eating bark off rotting timber after a cave-in or pouring gasoline on one's wounds to purge maggots.

These survivors are the defiant ones who refuse to give in to bad breaks or bad people that threaten their life. These survivors are the defiant ones who never say die.

ESCAPE FROM GROUND ZERO

"This just in. A plane has hit the North Tower of the World Trade Center!"

Dr. Gregory Fried, a New York Police Department chief surgeon, was stuck in traffic on the Long Island Expressway and was listening to the 8:45 A.M. traffic report on his car radio when the shocking news broke.

The 55-year-old physician immediately turned on his police scanner, now crackling with the tense voices of police dispatchers relaying rapid-fire reports to other members of the department. At 9:06 A.M. he heard "A second plane has just slammed into the South Tower! It's definitely a terrorist attack!"

Fried needed to be at Ground Zero because he knew there would be thousands of casualties. What he didn't know was that he would be one of them.

The Greatest Survivor Stories Never Told

Weaving through traffic with his siren blaring, Fried was about 10 miles from the city when he caught his first glimpse of the 110-story Twin Towers. The top floors were engulfed in flames and spewing huge plumes of black smoke.

At about 9:45 A.M. he parked a couple of blocks away from the WTC. He recalled that back in 1993, when the towers were rocked by a terrorist's car bomb, the area near the buildings became so packed with emergency vehicles that no one could get through, not even ambulances carrying the badly injured. Rather than add another car to the mess, he abandoned his vehicle. He grabbed his medical bag and donned his blue jacket emblazoned with big yellow letters POLICE on the back and NYPD on the front.

Fried pushed through crowds of shocked onlookers and soot-covered office workers—many dazed, crying, and gagging—who were running from the towers. He flagged down an emergency service van and hitched a ride to Ground Zero. The van was filled with young cops, most getting their first taste of a major disaster. Some would not survive the day.

As they headed for the WTC, they noticed papers and chunks of building materials fluttering down. Then a larger, heavier object slammed into the ground next to the van. "What the hell was that?" asked one of the cops.

Escape from Ground Zero

Fried peered out the window and winced. "That was a person," he said grimly.

It was then they realized the horror that was unfolding around them. Hundreds of doomed people were trapped on the top floors above the point of impact of the plane crashes. They were beyond rescue and knew they were going to die. Their only choice was how—death by fire or death by jumping. Dozens chose the latter, escaping the flames by smashing windows and leaping more than 1,000 feet to their deaths.

Fried had seen many gory scenes in his years on the force, but this was beyond horrific. Right now, however, he had to forget the images of mangled bodies and instead concentrate on saving lives.

Just south of the WTC, Fried hustled to the temporary police and firefighting headquarters that had been set up. There he was given a helmet to shield himself from the debris—broken glass, concrete chunks and metal shards—that was raining down from the towers.

Dodging the hail of rubble as best he could, Fried ran into an old friend, Lieutenant Terri Tobin, who, like him, was a two-decade veteran of the force. She was hurrying to her car to put on her sneakers.

"Heels might be fashionable but they're no good in a disaster," she told him.

"Stay safe, Terri," he said, kissing her on the

cheek before they both rushed off. Fried continued toward the command center, where police and fire officials were directing the rescue operation from a staging area in an open-air plaza less than half a block from the Twin Towers. It seemed to be a relatively safe place to deal with the thousands of wounded that were expected to be dragged from the burning buildings.

Suddenly Fried spotted a firefighter in full gear lurching toward him. Blood was gushing from his armpit. "Help me! Help me! I'm in pain. I'm bleeding," the firefighter cried before crumbling to the ground.

Fried examined the wounded man and quickly determined that the blood was spurting from a severed artery. Knowing he would have to improvise to save the firefighter's life, Fried looked around for something he could use to tie off the flow of blood. *A shoelace,* he thought, and bent down to untie his shoes.

Then he heard a frantic Emergency Medical Service paramedic 10 yards away shout, "The building's coming down!" Fried raised his eyes just in time to see a large piece of metal slice through the paramedic, killing him instantly.

Before Fried had time to react, he heard a monstrous explosion. The South Tower was collapsing. Big chunks of concrete and metal were screaming down at him like a salvo of bombs. It was unreal, more like special effects in a war movie than an actual event. Fried stared in frozen astonishment, then snapped back to reality. *Those ain't feathers,* he said to himself. *Run, Greg, run!*

But to where? There was no place to run to that was safe. The plaza was all open, nothing shading it except the building that was now falling. Fried dashed to the only place that looked like it might serve as cover, a low wall, then fell to the ground and rolled into a ball. A voice from his childhood came back to him, recalling those exercises every schoolkid had learned during the Cold War: "Duck and cover." Like a good schoolboy, he covered his head, curled up in a fetal position, and closed his eyes.

All of a sudden he felt a tremendous wallop slam into his lower back, knocking the air out of him. His sharp gasps were drowned out by the deafening sounds of thunderous crashing, clattering, and shattering all around him. The roaring tumult was so loud and lengthy that it distracted him from the pain that seared across his back.

How long is this going to last? he asked himself as steel, glass, and pulverized wallboard relentlessly bombarded him. His eyes still shut, he tried to coil himself into a tighter ball, to make a smaller target for the plummeting pieces of debris that were cutting and bruising his defenseless body. Except for the first piece of rubble that had smashed into his back, he was tolerating the barrage, although a nagging thought crept into his mind: *When is the next one going to come down and cut me in half?*

The rain of terror stopped moments later, and it became eerily quiet. Nearby a voice was moaning, "Help me. Help me." Fried slowly opened his eyes. But he couldn't see a thing. It was pitch black. He blinked and rubbed his eyes. Still, he saw nothing.

Damn it. I'm blind! he thought. Hearing the plaintive voice calling for help, Fried shouted back, "I can't help you! I'm blind!"

How could I be blind? His heart racing, he leaned against the now-crumbled wall and went through a list of potential causes of blindness. First he wondered whether the city had been hit with an atom bomb and the white-hot explosion had melted his eyes, as had happened to so many victims in Hiroshima. *No, that's not it. I didn't see a flash of light. Maybe a piece of debris struck my head, causing my blindness.* His trembling hand reached up to touch the top of his helmet and felt his bare head instead. Then his fingers probed the helmet. All that was left was the rim with jagged edges pointing up, like the crown of a king. He took the helmet off his head and held it in front of his face, but he couldn't see it and tossed it away in frustration.

Okay, I'm blind, he thought. *How am I going to function in the world if I'm blind?* Always practical,

Escape from Ground Zero

Fried started figuring out ways to get around his disability. *Well, you've got computers that talk. You've got things you can dictate into.*

As he sat in the darkness and rubble struggling to breathe from the swirling dust that filled his nose and lungs, he was already making plans for how he would live without his sight. Then his heart skipped a beat. *Hey, is that a band of light?* He rubbed his eyes and squinted. *Yes, yes it is!* The sliver of light reminded him of the break of dawn. *I'm not blind after all!* Only then did Fried realize that the blackness came from the dust of the pulverized materials that were choking the sky.

The cloud of smoke and dust grew gradually lighter, until everything seemed coated with a chalky gray soot. Every breath he took was labored and difficult because the air was thick with floating grime. Through the haze he saw shadowy figures, other survivors moving slowly about in the distance. Fried looked down to the spot where he had left the injured firefighter. There was no sign of him—no helmet, no clothes, no blood. The firefighter had vanished, apparently blown away by the rush of air when the massive structure fell.

Grimacing in pain, Fried slowly stood up and did a quick diagnostic check of himself. His arms and legs were battered and bleeding but otherwise they seemed okay. Parts of his lower back and rear, where he had been struck the hardest, were throbbing in pain. His rear was swollen and as soft as an I.V. bag. Fried knew that meant real trouble—he was bleeding internally. He took off his belt and wrapped it tightly around his buttocks.

Although he was dizzy and disoriented, he had enough presence of mind to know he had to find a safer area. He started dragging himself toward several figures he saw through the haze. "I can't walk," Fried said out loud, hoping someone would help him.

A bewildered man came toward him. "We've got to get out of here," the man muttered, and then kept walking right past Fried.

Walk or die, Fried told himself. He glanced over to where the South Tower had been. He saw nothing but smoke and a huge, jagged triangular shape rising about 50 feet from the ruins. It was part of the tower's façade. *It's like "Planet of the Apes,"* he thought. Despite the pain burning in his back, he forced himself to trudge away from the rubble. *Walk or die, Greg.*

Heading west through the haze, he saw the Hudson River and New Jersey on the other side. He hobbled past a chapel to what was once a park. Now it was a rubble-strewn necropolis draped with broken bodies. He stumbled several times over the gray dusty landscape and waded through piles of crushed stone, metal, and glass that sometimes reached his armpits. *Walk or die,* he kept telling himself.

Escape from Ground Zero

He was so focused on reaching the river—yet he was still in shock—that he wasn't fully aware that behind him the North Tower was crashing down.

Trying to block the agony from his mind, he doggedly pushed onward toward the river, each step more painful than the last. He finally met two police captains he knew. "Where's the temporary headquarters?" Fried asked.

"Doc, you look terrible," one of them replied. "We've got to get you help."

"I don't think I'm that bad," Fried replied. Pointing to Ground Zero, he insisted, "We have to help these people."

Instead, the captains forced him onto a police harbor boat, which would take him to a hospital. As Fried lay in the bottom of the boat, he noticed the craft was practically empty. "Where is everybody?" he asked, feeling a bit annoyed because he figured he was getting preferential treatment.

"They're all dead," came the somber reply.

One of the passengers onboard was a firefighter writhing in agony from a broken leg; a bone was poking through the skin. Fried tried to get up so he could tend to the injured man but the doctor had no strength to reach the moaning firefighter. However, Fried's instincts as a physician were still strong so he started to deal with the only injured body he could reach—his own.

He knew he was hemorrhaging. In an attempt to compress the blood flow, he tried pressing his wounded side against the deck of the boat and also tightened his belt around his rear. He put his fingers on his wrist to take his pulse, and found it was almost twice the normal rate. All of a sudden, his pulse faded and he became very cold. *This is it,* he thought, *I can't feel my pulse anymore.*

As he lay dying in the boat, he saw a strange tunnel that he had never seen before. To him the tunnel was not the entry into the Hereafter. As a man of science, he believed it was a physical reaction caused by blood vessels constricting the retinal artery. While staring into the tunnel, he heard voices ordering him, "Don't go out on us, Doc! Don't go out on us!"

"I'm not," he uttered feebly.

Fifteen minutes later, the boat reached the other shore, where he was loaded into an ambulance and transported to a New Jersey hospital. As he was wheeled into the emergency room, Fried, now on the verge of losing consciousness, asked, "Doc, am I going to die?"

Looking at the seriousness of Fried's injuries, the physician replied honestly, "I don't know."

@ @ @

Lieutenant Terri Tobin arrived at the horrific scene shortly after the first plane had slammed into the North Tower. Smoke was belching from the building and flames were shooting out the broken windows. Shaken workers were pouring out of the building as shattered glass, charred paper, and bits of furniture rained down on them.

Tobin coughed from the air thick with jet fuel and ash. Sirens wailed as people ran into the streets, their hair burned off, their clothes blackened by soot. Others, crying in pain, hobbled outside, their torn clothes revealing compound fractures as arm bones and leg bones stuck out of their dust-covered skin.

Tobin raced to the corner of Church and Vesey streets, where the NYPD had established a command center; now, command staff were dispersing police officers to various posts. On the advice of First Deputy Commissioner Joe Dunne, Lieutenant Tobin grabbed a strong, bullet-proof Emergency Services Unit helmet and put it on. It would later save her life.

She wondered what had caused the plane to crash—a terrible accident or a terrorist attack?—and she quickly learned the answer at 9:06 A.M., when the second plane smashed into the South Tower, setting off another huge explosion. Now she knew better. This was not some isolated tragedy. This was war.

She looked up at the North Tower and felt sick to her stomach. People trapped in the top floors and refusing to be burned alive were instead jumping to their deaths. *I can't imagine what a hell it must be for them,* she thought. *What an awful way to die.* By the dozens they fell—some already burned, some holding hands, some diving headlong to their deaths.

She cringed at the sight. Then she dashed into the North Tower to assist the uniformed personnel who were evacuating distraught office workers, secretaries, traders, and businesspeople who were streaming down the stairs. She wanted to make sure that the pathway out of the building was clear and that no unauthorized people were in what police refer to as the "frozen zone."

While the officers were directing people to safety, Lieutenant Tobin crossed over to the South Tower and saw a photographer taking photos of people coming down the escalator. Because he was impeding the evacuation and shouldn't have been there, Tobin escorted him out of the building to Church and Liberty streets.

It's going to be a long day, she told herself. *I'd better change into my sneakers.* She had parked nearby, and she hurried toward her car. She stopped briefly for a 10-second exchange with her good friend, Dr. Gregory Fried, and then scampered to her car. It was 10 A.M.

As she popped the trunk to get her sneakers, she heard a loud, ominous, rumbling noise behind her. She turned and started to walk back toward the South Tower when she met an onslaught of panicked people running toward her, screaming, "The building is coming down! Look out! Run for your lives!"

Tobin looked up and couldn't believe what she was seeing. The South Tower had already begun to pancake down. Before she had time to think, the force of 100,000 tons of steel and 200,000 cubic yards of concrete collapsing on each other blew Tobin literally out of her shoes. The hurricane-like force of the implosion threw her at least thirty feet into the air and onto the west side of West Street and Liberty where she landed facedown on the small grassy area in front of One World Financial Center.

As she lay still trying to get her bearings, her ears rang from the reverberating thunder of the tower's destruction compounded by several deafening explosions. *Oh God, we're being bombed!* she thought. Through the clamorous din she heard terrified voices crying out for help, for God, for anyone who could lead them away from this hell.

Huge chunks of falling debris pounded the ground around her as she scrunched her body as tightly as possible. *When will it stop? My God, it's falling all around me! Please, not on me . . .*

Suddenly, a heavy piece of plunging rubble clobbered her in the back of her head with such force that her helmet split in half and fell off. Nearly knocked out by the blow, the dazed and battered lieutenant tried to move but at first she couldn't.

Blood was oozing down her neck and when she put her hand to the back of her head, she felt a huge piece of cement still embedded in her skull. *Oh no, I'm hit! I'm hit! I wonder how bad it is.*

Then everything went totally black and totally silent. *I must be unconscious. I can't see. I can't hear. But am I really unconscious or is this a dream? No this is real, much too real.*

For minutes her mind remained woozy as she lay curled up on the ground—until she began coughing and realized it was extremely difficult to breathe. Every time she inhaled, she sucked in thick dust and hacked it out until her stomach hurt. She pulled her blouse up to cover her nose and mouth.

As the choking, black smoke started to clear, Tobin was able to make out the silhouette of a firefighter who called out to her, "Are you okay?"

"Yes, I think so," she said, still in shock.

"Don't move and keep your nose and mouth covered."

Tobin heard someone moaning next to her under a pile of rubble. She reached out and felt fingers poking out of the debris. As she grabbed the cold, clammy fingers, Tobin shouted to the person buried under the debris, "I'm a lieutenant with NYPD and there's a firefighter to my right and we'll help you. Don't move and try to cover your mouth and nose."

The air was heavy and her eyes and throat were burning. As the blackness began to lift, Tobin told the person whose hand she was holding, "I'm going to try to see if I can get up, but I won't let go of your hand."

Tobin was enmeshed in building cables and half-buried wire, under chunks of concrete. She struggled to get untangled and soon was able to get the top half of her body out of the rubble. As she wriggled loose, she realized that the hand she was holding had come free too easily. When she looked down, she gasped in horror. She was grasping a hand that was attached to an arm—but without a body. Tobin dropped the arm and frantically dug around the ruins, but she was unable to find the rest of the body.

When she stood up unsteadily, she turned around and saw that her car was being consumed in flames as were the ambulance and fire truck next to it.

She met two Emergency Medical Service workers, who gave her saline solution to wash out her eyes and clean out the black soot that coated her mouth and throat. She thought she spit out a piece of cement, only to discover it was one of her wisdom teeth. The EMS workers wrapped her head in gauze to stop the bleeding.

Tobin had barely survived the havoc from the collapse of the South Tower. But she was about to face another test of survival.

Shortly before 10:30 A.M., Tobin and other rescue workers were scrambling over the rubble, trying to trace the source of muffled cries for help from victims trapped underneath the ruins. She began digging and shoving rubble aside and pulling out trapped fellow rescue workers. She was busy helping others to safety and never even considered that the North Tower would come down too. But it did.

In fact, she was so engrossed in her efforts to save lives that she didn't hear the first forbidding sounds of the tower's collapse. When it started to topple onto itself, she heard people screaming, "The tower's coming down! Get out! Get out!"

Tobin started to run, but found it extremely painful because she had badly injured her ankle. Hobbling as fast as she could, which wasn't fast at all, she was quickly swallowed up by another black cloud of dust and debris.

Seconds later, a flying object struck her hard in the back between her shoulder blades, knocking her to the ground. Whatever it was felt sharp and had dug deep into her back. *Don't stay here!* she told herself. *Get out or you'll be buried again. You might not be so lucky this time.* Despite the pain in her back and her ankle, Tobin struggled to her feet and stumbled through the suffocating dust into a nearby apartment building. It had lost its power, and she followed the emergency lights on the ground floor. She opened the door to the stairwell and discovered at least a hundred terrified people huddled and blocking the stairs.

"Get out of the stairwell and into the lobby, but stay away from the glass windows!" she ordered. *Keep them calm,* she told herself. *Keep them moving.* After the people had been herded into the lobby, Tobin opened the door to the outside. It was surreal. Everything was gray—the sky, the rubble, the nearby buildings, the air itself. Pulverized cement had coated the world.

Two members of the NYPD Technical Assistance Response Unit arrived and told Tobin that they were evacuating people by boat to New Jersey.

One of the officers looked at her in disbelief. "Lieutenant, there's a big piece of glass sticking out of your back between your shoulder blades! You need medical attention immediately."

"We have to take care of these people first," she said.

"You need help now. You can't stay here. I'll go to the boat with you while the others begin evacuating the building."

When she arrived at the dock, two EMS workers cut her blouse off and gently pulled the glass shard from her back. They poured peroxide over the wound and dressed it with gauze. She was put aboard a boat that took her and other survivors to Ellis Island where she was then taken by ambulance to a medical center in New Jersey.

@ @ @

Lieutenant Terri Tobin and her friend Dr. Gregory Fried were among the survivors of America's darkest day.

Although it was touch and go for a few days in the hospital, Fried pulled through. He suffered three spinal fractures and had all the muscles ripped from his back. But he was able to go home on crutches ten days after the attack.

Meanwhile, Tobin was rushed into surgery, where doctors took a chunk of cement out of her head and stitched the wound, used eighty stitches to close the wound between her shoulder blades, and treated her for a fractured ankle, lacerations, and a severe concussion.

"You're lucky to be alive," the doctor told her.

"I couldn't agree with you more," Tobin replied.

A medic offered her a macabre souvenir—the concrete chunk, still covered with her blood and matted blond hair, that had been taken out of her scalp. Tobin stared at it for a moment, and said, "That's the last thing I want to have."

Escape from Ground Zero

After nearly two months of recuperation, Tobin returned to work. But just days later, she was shaken by more tragedy when a jetliner, American Airlines Flight 587 heading for the Dominican Republic, crashed into the Queens neighborhood of Belle Harbor—right in front of her house. All aboard were killed, as were five of her neighbors. Although parts of a jet engine landed on her front lawn and the house across the street was destroyed, her home was unscathed.

Tobin, a devout Roman Catholic, believes her close shaves with death were more than luck. "I think I had a guardian angel looking after me," she said. "Otherwise, why am I still here?"

THE WALKING MUMMY

In the middle of 1905 Pablo Valencia was struck with the fever and went mad.

No infection of the blood caused it, but the fever was strong, and it had been known to drive civilized men wild-eyed into the wilderness. Some died of it; others in its grip became crazed nomads, wandering desperately from one of the world's miserable isolated outposts to another.

The fever was *oro*—gold—and that summer it was raging in Pablo Valencia. Like a man possessed, he forgot everything, dropped everything and headed into the Arizona desert under the wilting August sun. He thought he had discovered the trail to the gold-laden "Lost Mines," and was hungry to seize their purported treasure.

But his odyssey ultimately took him to the very edge of hell, past the known limits of human tolerance and into the medical netherworld of the living dead.

The Greatest Survivor Stories Never Told

About noon on Monday, August 14, 1905, Pablo, a handsome, well-built 40-year-old Mexican, rode into the lonely camp of Dr. William McGee. The doctor was a man of science and medicine who was camping in this godforsaken part of the world to examine weather and the effects of light on the few creatures who made their homes in a place where there was not much more than sand and heat.

Dr. McGee and his assistant, Jose, had spent three months in relative isolation with infrequent visits from colleagues and passing prospectors at a place called Tinajas Atlas, 75 miles southeast of Yuma, Arizona, near the tip of the Sonora Desert. His camp was one of the few watering holes along a thoroughfare known as El Camino del Diablo—the Devil's Highway. After Death Valley it was the deadliest expanse of sand in the United States.

A half century earlier, this place had been one of the most treacherous stretches on the long road west for pioneers pushing to California. The road was dotted with stones and small crosses marking the graves of the weak ones who had died of thirst before reaching the next well, which was more than 20 miles away.

Along with Pablo rode another man, Jesus Rios, a sixty-five-year-old former cowboy who also had been struck with gold fever and was acting as Pablo's guide. Jesus was an unfortunate choice as a desert navigator, Dr. McGee noticed, because his grasp of the local geography—in fact, his memory in general—appeared to be completely unreliable.

The doctor took special note of Pablo, a former sailor who grew watermelons on a ranchita near Gila City in southwestern Arizona, when he wasn't chasing gold. Dr. McGee thought the five-foot-seven-inch, 155-pound prospector was one of the most robust men he had ever seen: vigorous and muscular, a big eater and a sound sleeper. Although he had a horse that had been well trained to work in the desert, Pablo preferred walking to riding and often trekked without his sandals. He was the kind of man who could doze off at the first sign of shade, but could then leap up and work nonstop for hours through the hottest part of the day if he thought his labors would bring him a single gold nugget.

Over a dinner of mountain sheep meat (a dish called jerked cimarron), bread, and cheese, Pablo and Jesus outlined the plans for their search for the "Lost Mines." Dr. McGee suggested that the men wait to start their journey until just after midnight when the moon would be at its brightest. The two men were intent upon leaving right away and departed quickly around five P.M. However, it wasn't long before they were back again. They said their horses were thirsty, but in reality they had realized that they should heed the doctor's advice.

At about four A.M. Tuesday they were off, and Dr. McGee believed he would not see them again for some time. He was wrong. Jesus Rios returned twenty hours later, around midnight, riding his own horse and leading his companion's steed. But where was Pablo?

"Pablo went ahead on foot to stake his claims and sent me back with the horses to get water," Jesus told Dr. McGee. "We are to meet up later on the far side of a sierra off the trail."

"But that's insane," Dr. McGee declared. "You might never find him."

Jesus shrugged his shoulders. He ate some food, watered the horses, and struck out on the trail at 3:30 A.M. Wednesday.

About seven A.M. Thursday, Jesus returned to the camp alone with both horses. "I looked all over," he told Dr. McGee. "But I couldn't find Pablo or any of his tracks. There's no sign of him anywhere."

Hoping to locate Pablo, Dr. McGee sent out his assistant, Jose, an expert in finding lost men in the desert. Jose spent a full day searching for Pablo's tracks or for any sign of the missing prospector, but he found no trace of the man.

It was now clear that Pablo was lost in the desert—an environment where healthy men have been known to dry up and die within a day.

By Friday morning, Dr. McGee was certain that

The Walking Mummy

Pablo had suffered the same fate as the hundreds of unfortunate pioneers who lay beneath the rough-hewn markers along the road. He had been gone for three days and had been carrying only one day's supply of water; no one could survive that long under the parching desert sun. Dr. McGee knew that half of all victims of thirst on the desert die within 36 hours of their last drink of water and another quarter die within 48 hours. Virtually all of those lost in the desert succumb within 80 hours if they can't get water.

The doctor was sure that Pablo was dead. But the doctor was wrong.

Around the time all were giving up hope, Pablo was still alive and wandering, as he had been for more than two full days since Tuesday night, when he and his partner had gone in different directions. Jesus had gone back to Dr. McGee's camp with the horses and the water. Pablo went on foot alone. He had only a two-gallon canteen of water, some food, tobacco, a hammer, and a specimen bag.

Jesus had given him directions to a road that was supposed to take him to their rendezvous spot. At first secure in the idea that he and Jesus would arrive at the designated place, Pablo went on with his work, staking markers for mineral claims and gathering specimens.

In the early afternoon on Wednesday he started to

head north to the meeting spot, which intersected with a road that headed farther into the desert. He walked and walked, carefully following the directions Jesus had given him. No road ever appeared, however. There was just sand, an endless shimmering expanse of sand.

By Thursday his canteen was almost empty, even though he had been trying to preserve his supply by swishing the water around in his mouth but not swallowing. Nevertheless, the last drop was gone by the end of that day, and for the first time in a long time, Pablo stopped thinking about gold.

Withering under the desert sun, he trudged ever so slowly. Every ounce of gear and supplies that he carried seemed to weigh a ton. He tossed off his serape and discarded what little food he had left and even dumped the few gold nuggets he had. But he kept his canteen.

All he could think about was water.

His mouth feeling as though it was coated with sand and his lips cracked, the desperate man was forced to rely on the only liquid he knew for sure was available—his own urine. He relieved himself into his canteen and then gargled with his own urine. It offered little relief but it was still better than no moisture at all. He saved every drop of urine in his canteen. During the blazing heat of the day, he huddled in an arroyo and tried to eat some wild gourds he had found. But they were of no use, and only made him throw up.

When night fell, he started to search for the road again, continuing north. Walking became increasingly difficult, so he sought to lighten his load by dumping his sandals, then his pants, which held his money, a knife, and tobacco. These might have been useful in his fight for survival, but he didn't care. All he knew was that they were too heavy to carry through the desert heat.

He had wandered for nearly four days, three with no liquid except for his own urine, when to his exhilaration a trail appeared. It was there, clearly marked, he was sure of it. With quick steps and rapid breath, he moved along, expecting at any moment to see Jesus and the horses—and life-saving water. Faster and faster he walked, his heart pounding with happy anticipation. Then like black magic the trail vanished, disappearing into a wall of rock. Wildly he groped about, then picked up the trail again on the other side of the rock and staggered along, until it vanished a second time.

Then the truth dawned on him. There had never been a trail. In his feverish desperation, he had imagined it. It was just a mirage.

Dejected, Pablo swished urine around in his mouth, continued to walk north for a few miles, then curled up under a small paloverde tree to wait for the heat of day to fade. He munched on a couple of bugs and chewed some morsels of mescal cactus, which yielded a few precious drops of moisture. But it was getting harder and harder for him to swallow.

At nightfall on Friday, he listlessly pushed on, even though he knew he was dying. *Where did I go wrong?* he wondered as he stumbled onward. Pablo mulled over the directions Jesus had given, backtracking in his mind every step, going over everything that had happened in the past few days.

It was then that Pablo began to suspect that Jesus had steered him in the wrong direction on purpose. Jesus had never intended to meet him at all. Instead, Pablo realized, Jesus had planned to leave him to die in the desert so Jesus could make off with all the gold. Pablo imagined the older man filling his purse with gold, and he grew angry, then enraged. *No matter what,* he promised himself, *I am going to make it back, just so I can have the pleasure of plunging a knife into that old buzzard's heart.*

Spurred on by thoughts of murder, Pablo took another slug of urine and pressed on. Now his luck turned. He came upon a new road, and this time it was no figment of his imagination. It was the Old Yuma Trail, a main thoroughfare for pioneers traveling west, but a road dotted with graves. He knew that it would help lead him back to Dr. McGee's camp 19 miles away. But in his condition, it might as well have been 1,900 miles.

Early Saturday morning, Pablo found a fat scorpion, which he ate after crushing the creature with a rock. He washed it down with urine and then moved on, until the heat once again forced him to seek shelter in a shaded gully.

Now that he had some idea of where he was, his daydreams jumped between killing Jesus and reaching a famed old watering hole—the thirty-seven-foot-deep Tule Well, located two miles off the trail—and tossing himself into the cool mud at the bottom. These motivating thoughts spurred him on with a steel will to survive even if it meant catching and eating bugs and drinking his own urine.

But soon he was much too dehydrated to urinate anymore. The last drop of the only liquid that had sustained him, his urine, was consumed.

Pablo was losing the battle, and the desert seemed to know it. Coyotes started following him and buzzards circled overhead as they awaited his death. Soon the weakening, delusional prospector's perceptions became frighteningly out of whack. In the distance the mountains were changing shape and swaying to and fro. Cacti uprooted themselves and danced in front of him. Still, Pablo refused to give up, pushing on past the dancing cacti and toward the undulating mountains.

His tenacity to survive was fueled solely by the sweet images of the tip of his knife penetrating Jesus' chest, the blood coming first in drops, then gushing out as the old double-crosser died a slow, painful death.

During his trek toward the camp, Pablo kept seeing the place with a full canteen waiting for him just a few yards ahead of him. He kept hearing the rumble of wagon wheels and the sounds of horses. But when he rubbed his eyes and ears, he saw and heard nothing. Only sand and buzzards.

As the sun rose on Sunday, the sixth day, Pablo said a prayer for just a little more strength, just a little more time to live. He saw the buzzards flying in tighter circles directly overhead. They knew, as he did, that time was running out. At one point while he was resting, Pablo felt his soul leave his body and float over his own corpse. But he wasn't dead. Not yet, at least.

The next day, he could hardly walk, so he crawled and shuffled for several miles until he came to a trail that headed straight for Dr. McGee's camp. He was only a few miles away, but he had run out of energy. His body seemingly had nothing left to give. Ready to concede, Pablo stretched himself across the trail so rescuers wouldn't miss finding him when he died. As he lay down, the last sight he saw before closing his eyes were the buzzards landing and staring at him only a few feet away.

The Walking Mummy

When he awoke several hours later, he was pleasantly startled to discover that he was still alive. Somehow his energy had been recharged, although barely.

It was now Tuesday, the eighth day since the prospector had left Dr. McGee's camp; the fifth day since the last drop of water had trickled down his throat. Pablo knew that if he didn't reach the camp today, he would never make it. He tried so hard to walk, but after taking a few steps he tumbled to the dusty ground. All he could do was creep ever so slowly on his hands and knees over rocks and through the thorny clumps on the trail.

By nightfall, his body had nothing left to give. It was shutting down. No amount of willpower could move it another foot. He crumpled to an arroyo below the Mesa of the Forty Graves just short of reaching Dr. McGee's camp. Pablo knew it was time for him to give up. He faced east, made the sign of the cross, and uttered a final prayer. His only regret was that he had no consecrated water

As if in a hazy dream, he felt his naked body heaving and he heard a feeble voice cry out for help, but it didn't sound anything like his own. Then he drifted off for what he was sure was his last minutes on earth.

Back at the camp, Dr. McGee was awakened early Wednesday to an odd sound, a mournful wail that reverberated off the canyon walls in the still morning air. "It must be Pablo," Dr. McGee said to Jose. "Get the canteen."

They walked for about a quarter mile. There they found the lost prospector lying under an ironwood tree surrounded by grave markers. He wasn't moving. The robust, healthy Mexican of eight days ago now looked like a dried-up, leathery, dark-skinned mummy. Pablo was stark naked; his formerly full-muscled legs and arms were shrunken and scrawny; his ribs ridged out like those of a starving horse; his normally bulky abdomen had collapsed almost against his vertebral column.

Dr. McGee assumed Pablo was dead, but then the prone figure emitted a weak groan. "My God, he's alive! He's *alive*!" Dr. McGee shouted, much to his and Jose's astonishment.

The doctor immediately splashed water on the parched man because he could not swallow. Pablo's skin absorbed the water as greedily as a dry sponge. His skin was black, dotted with patches of gray and purple and crisscrossed with cuts and scratches— none of which were bleeding because he had so little fluid in his body.

His lips had disappeared, leaving only a ridge of dry, blackened skin out of which his teeth protruded like those of a skinned animal. Where his tongue should have been there was a small, wrinkled chunk of black flesh like a raisin pasted to his teeth. Dr. McGee could not find a pulse, and Pablo's eyes—sunken, glassy, and staring—had trouble focusing. It was as if he had already died, and was only waiting for his body to catch up with him.

But Pablo was still breathing with a weird, rasping moan. It was that very act of a dying man struggling to take a breath that, from a distance and amplified by a desert gorge, had reached the ears of the doctor.

After dousing the prospector with water, Dr. McGee and Jose carried him back to the camp. There the physician gave him a powerful heart stimulant and forced a few slugs of whiskey and coffee down his throat. Within a few hours Pablo was eating a few bites of a fricassee of bird and rice. A short time later, he spoke his first word. *"Agua, agua,"* he gasped. He had spent eight agonizing days in the desert, nearly seven without water. He had lost 25 pounds, and his hair, which had been black at the start of his ordeal, had turned completely gray.

Within a day he was gaining his strength, his skin softened, and his circulation returned to normal. Two days later, he told Dr. McGee of the horror he endured over the previous week. Then his eyes grew wide and, referring to Jesus, he snarled, "Where is that bastard?"

"He left several days ago," Dr. McGee replied.

"Once he learns you're alive, I don't think you'll be able to find him. He'll be long gone." Eventually Pablo abandoned his plan to murder the conniving—and missing—Jesus.

Pablo's survival and recovery astounded Dr. McGee so much that he wrote a detailed paper about it, called "Desert Thirst as Disease," for a medical journal in 1906. His paper is still read today in the Southwest.

As for Pablo, two months after his recovery he was ready to venture out into the desert again. This time, he chose to travel with a more reliable and honorable guide.

CRISIS IN THE MONKEY HOLE

Coal miners David Fellin and Hank Throne were helplessly trapped by a cave-in in a cramped underground chamber of darkness and doubt, completely cut off from the outside world.

Day after day they waited in silence and isolation, wondering, hoping, praying that on the surface 330 feet above rescuers would find them and pluck them from their pitch-black tomb before it was too late—before they succumbed to hunger, suffocation, flash flood, poisonous gas, another cave-in, or even raging madness.

On Tuesday morning, August 13, 1963, Fellin, 58, who had been scrabbling for a living in the slag-strewn anthracite country of eastern Pennsylvania most of his life, and Throne, 28, who was new on the job, headed down the shaft with a veteran miner, Louis Bova, 54. Co-owned by Fellin, the mine near Hazelton was, like many in the region, a tiny operation that wasn't required to meet certain rigid safety standards. Also like many small mines, it had just one entry.

Fellin had experienced a weird feeling shortly after they reached the bottom of the shaft. He couldn't quite figure out what it was, but it seemed as though his body was trying to tell him something. "Boys," he told his fellow miners, "my stomach is a little out of whack. Let's go out for an hour or so."

But the other two persuaded him to stay. In a cavern near the bottom of the mine, they began carving their way toward what they hoped was a rich coal vein. They filled a buggy, a small cart for carrying coal on a track, and sent it up to the surface, where a fourth worker, George Walker, emptied it. While waiting for the buggy to return, Bova was standing on one side of the track, Fellin and Throne on the other. All three froze when they heard the first terrifying sounds of impending disaster.

It started as a small trickle of falling rock, followed by a low rumble that grew louder by the second. The miners knew what was coming . . . and there was nothing they could do to stop it. "Cave-in!"

The 12-foot-by-12-foot shaft, which sloped 82 degrees from the surface, was collapsing on itself. The timbers on the walls and ceiling cracked and tumbled to the floor. Then, with a thunderous roar, big chunks of rock and coal crashed down wildly around the men as they ducked for cover. Through the thick dust and rubble, Fellin and Throne caught a brief glimpse of Bova cowering on the other side of the track.

The cave-in came in violent, ear-pounding, throat-choking waves between periods of eerie calm that lasted about 30 seconds. After several scary minutes, the deadly torrent of rock had subsided. But then the electrical line that powered the work lights snapped, plunging the men into darkness.

"Did he cut the power? Did he cut it?" Fellin shouted anxiously, hoping Walker, up at the surface, was smart enough to take such action. Fellin knew that live wires could short out, sparking a fire that would mean an agonizing death in minutes. The old miner held his breath, his heart thumping, and waited for flames to flare. But it remained dark and quiet, except for an occasional clattering of a falling rock.

Fellin and Throne turned on their helmet lamps. By the dim light they surveyed their "monkey hole"—mining jargon for a small chamber or air pocket. It was about six feet by five feet and only three feet high. The floor of the cavern was tilted so that it was higher at one end and lower at the other. A jumble of rocks and timbers from floor to ceiling separated them from Bova.

"Lou! Lou! Are you okay?" Fellin shouted.

From behind the blockage, about 20 feet away, came Bova's faint voice. "Davy, Hank. I think I hurt my hip." Then he fell silent.

"Don't fret," Fellin told him. "We'll try to find a way out." But he knew it was hopeless. Because the mine was small, it was exempt from federal regulations that required two exits. Now the sole exit, the only way out, was blocked by tons of dirt and rock.

Their lunch pails, picks, shovels, and other tools were buried under the debris. As their helmet lamps grew dimmer, they hurriedly rummaged through the rubble and salvaged a plastic jug half full of water, a mason hammer, a hatchet, a four-foot pipe, some cable, and some rags. By the time they had gathered the items, their lights flickered out.

They were now prisoners in a subterranean jet-black world.

Together the two men sat in the cold darkness, straining to hear for more rushes, the tell-tale sounds of a cave-in. For more than half a day, they barely moved or spoke as they pondered their plight and sipped water from the jug.

Fellin knew that it could be days or weeks before searchers could find them—dead or alive. If they had any chance of survival, they needed more water.

"Listen," Throne said. From the lower level of their chamber they heard *drip, drip, drip*. They felt around blindly in the dark and discovered a drainage hole in the floor of the shaft below the blockage. They dropped a pebble and listened for its splash; they figured the pool of water was about 10 feet down. Now that they had found water, the next challenge was getting it.

Fellin had a brainstorm. Groping in the dark, he collected some of the items that they had gathered before their lamp lights went out. He ran the cable through the pipe and made a knot on the lower end and plugged that end with rags. He lowered the pipe into the drainage hole, let it fill with water, and pulled it up.

Carefully, he poured the precious liquid into the plastic jug and took a gulp. He gagged and spit it out. Throne tried it too, with the same reaction. It was sulfur water, a nauseating acrid liquid that flowed through the mines.

"Yeah, it's bad, but it's water and it'll keep us alive," Fellin told Throne. "Take it a quarter swallow at a time. At least we won't get any belly aches."

Fellin's joke wasn't lost on his companion. In a diluted form, sulfur water was an old folk remedy, a spring tonic for children who ate too many green apples.

On the second day, they crawled around in the blackness feeling for any kind of opening that might give them a chance to escape. But there was none.

Fellin tried to picture how the rescue operation was going at the surface. *Why haven't we heard any drilling yet? What's taking them so long? Do they have any clue where we are?* Then he thought about his wife, Anna. *I wonder how she's bearing up, if she's getting any sleep.*

"Dear Lord, help us get out. Please help us," Throne prayed over and over. He thought about his wife and twin girls and the guys he hung around with at Anne's Café in Hazelton. And he thought about guzzling a beer.

The temperature in the clammy cave dropped below 40° as the cold seeped deep into their bones. To keep warm, Fellin would sit with his legs spread out, with Throne leaning his back against Fellin's chest. Fellin would breathe on Throne's neck and back and rock him back and forth. Then they would switch places.

They tried repeatedly to contact Bova on the other side of the wall of debris, but after a few feeble knocks of rock against rock during the first day, they heard nothing more from him.

Sleep was almost out of the question for Fellin. He wanted to stay alert so he wouldn't miss the sounds he hoped for, the drilling of a rescue hole, or the sounds he feared, the crashing of a cave-in. Besides, it was hard for him to nod off when he was shivering, hungry, and uneasy. Throne tried to forget about his predicament by sleeping as much as he could.

Days passed—though they weren't sure how many—as they waited and wondered what fate had in store for them. Death or rescue?

It was during this difficult time of loneliness, darkness, and silence—when the brain is void of the usual billions of sensory signals it receives continuously from the outside world—that the two miners began hallucinating. They were seeing strange lights and human figures. The two men were convinced that what they were seeing was real because, amazingly, they were both witnessing the same things at the same time.

One day, Fellin excitedly whispered to Throne, "Hank, do you see that?"

"Yeah, it's a man with a helmet light. He's facing away from us."

"That's what I see, but he doesn't seem real. He scares me down to my toes."

Ignoring Fellin's fear, Throne hollered to the figure, "Hey, Buddy! How about showing me some light over here!"

But the figure kept his light aimed away from the miners. As Throne crawled toward him, the figure moved away and vanished.

More than once, the miners saw a door rimmed in blue light leading to gleaming marble steps.

"Imagine that, a door at the bottom of a mine," Throne marveled. It then vanished.

Throne and Fellin continued warming each other with their breath and sipping their sulfur cocktails, which had started to go down more smoothly. The miners were getting alarmed because five smaller cave-ins had lowered parts of the height of their monkey hole to a claustrophobic 18 inches.

On the surface, rescue workers were frustrated and pessimistic. Every time they tried to break through the debris in the main shaft, they were driven back by poisonous gases known as "black damp." More cave-ins hampered their efforts too.

As hope of the miners' survival dwindled, Fellin's brother Joe, a veteran miner, convinced the rescue workers to try a long shot: drill a borehole to the chamber where the men were likely working when the mine collapsed Tuesday morning. It was now Friday. But exactly where that monkey hole was, no one was sure. Because Joe was familiar with the mine, rescue workers began drilling under his direction while the miners' families and hundreds of townspeople kept vigil at the site.

The drilling rig bored one hole, then another and another. But by Sunday morning, five days since the cave-in, the rescuers, now soaked from a nasty thunderstorm, still hadn't located the trapped miners.

Down below, the miners heard water flowing

through the rocks. "Davy, it's raining up top," Throne said. "It must be coming down pretty hard."

They both knew what that meant. Water seeping through the blocked shaft and onto the already unstable debris could touch off another major rock fall or it could back up and flood their cavern. Either way, it meant death.

For the first time since they were underground prisoners, Throne panicked. "Davy, I'm going home!" he screamed, crawling madly around in the dark. "I'm going alone if you don't want to come."

Fellin tried to calm him. "Now wait, Hank. We'll go together," he said. "But not right now. We have to be patient."

Eventually Throne came to his senses, realizing that the best thing he could do—in fact, the only thing he could do—was sit down, take a slug of sulfur water, and wait in the darkness. Fortunately, the heavy rain lasted only about 20 minutes, and soon the flow of water diminished much to the miners' relief.

Although Throne had managed to block out thoughts of food for days, he could no longer ignore the hunger pangs gnawing in his empty stomach. In desperation, he ripped off a piece of bark from an old rotted timber and chewed on it. The bark tasted bitter and hardly satisfying.

Later that day, Sunday, they were flabbergasted

when an unmistakable voice shattered the silence. After five days without a word or sound, Lou Bova, the other lost miner, was calling to them. "Davy, Hank, where are you? This is Louis."

"Lou, we're here! It's so great to hear you!" Fellin hollered in elated surprise.

"I've come to take you home," Lou yelled back.

Wondering what he meant, Fellin and Throne peppered him with questions. But despite repeated efforts, they failed to get a response from him.

Hours later, while still recovering from the shock of hearing from Louis, the two miners were startled again by a different voice: "Look for the light!"

Fellin and Throne dug frantically at the rubble, shoving and yanking rocks nonstop for two hours until . . . "I see a light!" Fellin gleefully shouted. This time when they moved toward the light, it didn't vanish. After clawing their way through six feet of debris that had separated them from another part of the cavern, they found a light dangling on a cord from a six-inch-wide hole. Also hanging from the hole was a microphone and a speaker calling their names. "Here we come! Here we come!" yelled Throne.

"What day is it?" Fellin asked as he reached the microphone.

"What day do you think it is?" a rescuer shouted back.

"Sunday," Fellin replied.

Crisis in the Monkey Hole

"That's right," the rescuer said. "It's late Sunday night."

"Then Throne is wrong, because he thought it was Monday," Fellin crowed. "Send us some soup."

In no time, bottles of barley soup and coffee and candy bars were lowered to the starving miners. One rescuer asked what they had been living on for the past six days.

"Sulfur water," Fellin replied, "I don't have any belly aches since I've been drinking this stuff." Flashlights, blankets, and tools followed, and once again the men were connected to the world.

Anna Fellin, who had been sitting and praying by the mine since the cave-in, was led over to the mike. "Dave, how are you?" she yelled down.

"I can hear you hollering all over," he shouted back. "I'm not sick or hurt. How are you?"

"I'm all right," she cried, tears trickling down her cheeks. "I love you."

"All right," Fellin said. "I'll talk to you later. I have work to do down here."

Although their rescue seemed imminent, Fellin and Throne knew their ordeal was far from over. The borehole wasn't wide enough for them to escape. Rescuers needed to drill a bigger hole, but when they tried, they ran into maddening failures by either missing the monkey hole or slamming into diamond-hard rock.

On the third day of new drilling, Fellin heard the ominous sound of rock shifting. He grabbed Throne's arm and hustled him to another part of the cavern just as the roof caved in. They had lost many supplies, but the hole and the light were still intact.

Fellin directed the boring of another hole, knowing that with every turn of the drill the danger increased of another cave-in. Finally on Friday August 23, the tenth day of their imprisonment, a 12-inch drill busted through the roof of the cavern. Fellin and Throne cheered and shook hands. They were almost free. Before they could be pulled up, however, the hole had to be reamed to 18 inches. That would take several more days.

At the same time, six-inch holes were being poked into the ground to locate Bova. Although there had been no word from him since the last odd contact the previous Sunday, Fellin and Throne were certain he was still alive because he most likely had access to sulfur water. Besides, Bova was a strong man known for marching around in the dead of winter without a coat.

Meanwhile, rescuers sent down timbers, boards, tools, and nails that the two trapped miners, now working 12 to 14 hours a day, used to shore up the monkey hole so that the constant vibration from the drill wouldn't cause a deadly collapse. Hour by hour the 65-ton drilling rig spun the reamer through the crumbling coal and shale above the miners' heads. To Fellin and Throne, the grinding of the cutting bit whistled, shrieked, and roared like a thousand locomotives.

As they toiled over the next three days, the veteran cracked jokes while the rookie sang his favorite songs, "Mona Lisa," "South of the Border," and "Do Not Forsake Me Oh My Darling." Hearing them joke and sing, the rescuers thought that for two men whose lives were still very much in peril, they seemed remarkably chipper.

On Monday evening, August 26, the reamer broke through the roof of their cavern. Down the widened hole came special coveralls with parachute harnesses sewn into them. After donning the clothes, the miners slathered each other with grease.

Fellin asked rescuers if there were many spectators up top. Assured there were thousands, he said, "Well, you better get some clothes pins because we stink like old goats."

Fellin ordered that Throne be hauled up first. "I can't go first," Fellin explained. "I'd crucify any guy who went ahead of an inexperienced man."

Throne attached his harness to a line from a hoist on the surface and at 1:53 A.M. Tuesday, was slowly pulled up. "Boy, what a ride this is!" he yelled. When he reached the surface 12 minutes later to wild cheers and fresh air, the black-dusted miner covered his eyes from the glare of the spot-light and shouted, "I'm out! I'm out!" Then he broke down and sobbed for the first time in two weeks.

At 2:31 A.M. Fellin began his ascent. On the way up, a rescue worker told him, "You've lost a little weight. You're coming up easy."

"Well, you don't eat too much down here," Fellin replied. As he neared the top, his voice rang out clear, "I can see light!" Then he burst into song. "She'll be coming 'round the mountain when she comes . . ."

The first person he saw when he reached the sur-face was his brother Joe, whose long-shot plan to save the miners had worked. Joe shook his hand and said, "Glad you're safe."

"Me too," said Fellin. It was the first time the two had spoken in 20 years.

Fellin and Throne were whisked to the hospital, where doctors found them to be in surprisingly good shape. By the second day of their freedom, the men were munching hamburgers, drinking beer, and smoking stogies.

Upon his release a week later, Fellin returned to the mine entrance where efforts were still under way to rescue Bova. "I've got to try to help out my buddy," Fellin declared. "We've got to find him."

Sadly, Bova's body was never recovered. The mine that entombed Fellin and Throne for two harrowing weeks had become their fellow miner's grave.

THE HITCHHIKE TO HELL

Tucked somewhere in the recesses of her mind were the words of older, wiser voices of parents and teachers warning her about the dangers of hitching rides with strangers. But Mary Vincent was 15 years old, in the throes of teenage rebellion, and raring for adventure and the freedom of the road.

So on the hot, muggy afternoon of September 29, 1978, the pretty teen with the long, curly, dark hair strolled along the shoulder of a road in Berkeley, California, and held out her thumb. She had planned on hitchhiking 400 miles south to visit her grandfather near Los Angeles.

She ended up hitchhiking to hell.

Mary had thumbed rides many times, ever since she dropped out of school in the ninth grade and began carving a devil-may-care life as a runaway. Her strict parents back in Las Vegas were heartbroken but couldn't figure out how to tame their wild daughter.

For a time Mary lived the West Coast Bohemian life, rummaging around during the day and sleeping with her 26-year-old boyfriend in his car in Sausalito. That lasted until he was arrested and charged with raping a high school girl unknown to Mary. So Mary was soon on the road again, this time on a freeway on-ramp thumbing her way to Grandpa's.

She never made it there.

Within minutes, a blue Ford van rolled to a stop. "Hop in," said the driver. He was a balding, middle-aged man in a blue jumpsuit stretched tight over a beer belly—a little creepy, but then, there were a lot of creeps on the road. She told him she was heading to the L.A. area. The driver said that although he was on his way to Reno, Nevada—200 miles northeast of Berkeley—he was willing to go out of his way to take her south to Los Angeles. So Mary plunked herself down in the seat next to the man who introduced himself as Larry.

As they drove off, Mary pulled out a cigarette and took a long drag. When that made her sneeze, Larry reached over and grabbed the back of her neck. He pulled her toward him, saying, "Let's see if you're sick."

"Stop it!" snapped Mary as she jerked away. Annoyed at being hit on so soon and so crudely, she pressed herself against the door to keep from his probing hands.

A few minutes later, Larry stopped at his house to pick up some bags of laundry. Although Mary was a runaway, she was still perilously naïve. Instead of bolting, the young traveler helped him load his bundles into the back of the van and then climbed in.

As they headed for I-5, which would take them south, she noticed that Larry was guzzling something from a milk carton as he drove. From the smell, Mary knew it wasn't milk. But she didn't think anything of it, and soon dozed off.

It was near dusk when her eyes fluttered open and she glimpsed the roadside signs. To her alarm, she realized the van was taking her northeast to Nevada. Panicked, she grabbed a sharp stick from the rear and pointed it at Larry. "Turn this van around right now!" she demanded.

Meekly, he did. "I made an honest mistake," he pleaded. "I'm not gonna hurt you."

Once they were southbound again, Mary put down the stick and relaxed. Larry, now reeking of whiskey, kept making stops along the road to relieve himself. After sunset, he turned off I-5 near Modesto and drove down a dark lonely road—a road that would lead Mary to the agony of unspeakable brutality.

He stopped the van in a remote area hidden from view because, he said, he had to relieve himself.

Mary did too, so she walked about 20 yards away in the opposite direction. Moments later, as she was tying her shoe, she felt a crushing blow across her back. Trying to catch her breath, she turned around and looked up just in time to see his fist slam into her face.

"Don't scream or I'll kill you," Larry snarled.

Reeling from the vicious blows, Mary didn't struggle as he carried her to the van and threw her in the back facedown. In a flash, he was on top of her. She felt his hulking body pressing down on her legs as he grabbed a piece of rope and tied her hands behind her back. Then he turned her over, ripped off her clothes and raped her. *The face, remember his face,* she told herself.

After the attack was over, he got behind the wheel and drove deeper into the desert, farther away from the lights of the freeway. "Let me go! Please, let me go!" she begged.

Minutes later, he stopped and untied her hands. "Get out," he ordered.

Finally, she thought, *he's going to set me free.*

He handed her a cup of whiskey. "Drink it or I'll kill you," he warned. She did what she was told. But then to her horror, he raped her again. In the mayhem swirling around her, though, she tried to remember every detail of his face.

When Larry finished assaulting her, he left her

naked and bruised on the side of the road. Numb from shock and pain, she didn't move. When she heard the van door open, Mary thought, *At last he's going to leave me alone.*

Mary was dead wrong. He returned, only this time he was waving an ax. "You want to be free?" he screamed as he grabbed her left hand. "I'll set you free!"

She tried to pull away, but he was too strong. With a whoosh, the ax came down on her left forearm—once, twice, three times until her limb fell to the ground. Blood spurted out. She screamed but there was no one to hear her. The ax came down again, this time on her right forearm. It took four blows to sever that limb.

Let me die, she thought. *Death can't be any worse.*

In a fury, the despicable monster picked up the bleeding girl and tossed her over a bridge and down an embankment. *Is it over now?* Mary wondered. It wasn't.

Larry scrambled to the gully where she had landed and picked her up again. "As soon as I leave, you'll be free," he sneered. Then he stuffed her into a dark, damp concrete drainage pipe. As he walked away, he told her, "Now you're free."

Don't move, Mary told herself. *Don't say a word. Play dead. Maybe he'll finally go away.* In agony and terror, Mary lay very still, alternately praying that he would leave and let her live or that she would simply die. Blood was gushing from her wounds. If she didn't stop the hemorrhaging, she knew she would die. *It'll be over soon and then I won't hurt anymore,* she thought. *Just let the blood flow out.*

But then deep within her, she felt a life-affirming surge from a basic human instinct—the need to survive.

Hearing the van roar off, she lay in the drainage pipe and held up what was left of her arms. Slowly the bleeding stopped. In shock and pain and weak from loss of blood, Mary dragged herself out of the pipe. About dawn she started walking, all the time holding up her stumps to prevent the bleeding from starting again and to keep her muscles from falling out.

The sun was up when she made it to a highway about three miles away and saw two young men in a red sports car. They slowed down, but when they saw the naked, armless, bloodied girl calling out to them from the shoulder of the road, the driver yelled to the passenger, "Let's get the hell out of here!" The car zoomed off as Mary cried out for them to come back.

She staggered along the road a while longer, growing weaker with each step, until she was discovered by a young couple, who brought the dying girl to a hospital. While doctors worked feverishly to save Mary's life, police waited anxiously to talk to her. In a few days, thanks to Mary's ability to pay attention to detail, they had a comprehensive description and a composite sketch of the man who had tried to kill her.

Within two weeks police arrested a suspect—Larry Singleton, a 51-year-old divorced merchant mariner. Singleton had been fingered by a neighbor when she saw the police sketch in the newspapers. The cops picked him up in Sparks, Nevada, where they also found two hatchets and, drying on a clothes line in the yard, carpeting from his van. It had been washed with soap and water. The clothes Mary had been wearing the night of the brutal attack were found in his fireplace. Singleton was charged with attempted murder, rape, forced oral copulation, sodomy, kidnapping, and mayhem. He pleaded innocent.

As difficult as it was to survive the attack, Mary needed to muster even more resolve to survive the challenges that lurked ahead.

By the time Singleton was arrested, Mary was fitted with prosthetic arms and was learning to tie shoes, feed herself, and write her name. It was hard at first, and she sometimes wanted to give up. But the physical therapist would have none of it.

"I can't do it, I won't do it, and I don't want to," Mary wailed.

"You can, you will, and you must," the therapist declared.

And Mary would try. But the emotional wounds ran deep. Night after night, she was haunted in her sleep by the grisly attack. Nurses often found her sleepwalking down the hallways, moaning loudly.

On her strong days in the hospital, she would tell the staff, "Jeez, I've got a long life to live. I don't want to rot here like a little vegetable." But on her weak days, she would confess, "I hate myself because I don't have my hands. It's like the end of the world for me."

At Singleton's trial six months after the assault, Mary faced her assailant and bravely relived the traumatic ordeal in court. Her gut-wrenching testimony convicted him. As she left the witness stand, he swore he would kill her. Although the judge said he wished he could send him to prison for the rest of his natural life, Singleton received a 14-year sentence, the maximum allowed by California law.

While her assailant was behind bars, Mary too felt imprisoned, confined in an emotional cage. Preoccupied by the monstrous attack, she became depressed and suicidal and suffered from recurring dreams that left her in a cold sweat.

Although Mary learned how to manipulate her artificial arms and metal hooks to cook, draw, and even bowl, there were times when it took her an hour or two just to get herself together in the morning because she couldn't stop crying. Her artificial limbs were constant reminders of the unimaginable horror she endured.

"I would do anything if I could have my hands back and be able to feel the softness of a puppy," she told a confidante. "I hate it when I start crying in front of everybody because it makes them cry. But I can't keep feeling sorry for myself. That just means you're not strong enough to live."

During those low periods, Mary pulled herself together by talking to God. She reminded herself that she had lived through something that would have killed most people. She was tough; she was a survivor. But those pep talks with herself didn't erase the harsh reality she had to face.

After finishing high school, Mary felt isolated. Her parents divorced and her old friends felt uncomfortable around her.

She tried doing lectures to high school students on the dangers of hitchhiking. It was frustrating because she realized that young people wouldn't take her advice. She knew—she had been there—but they wouldn't listen. "You got what you deserved!" one coldhearted teen yelled at her after she finished a speech. It was too much. She stopped trying to teach them the lesson she had so painfully learned, and withdrew from the world. She felt listless and depressed. Therapy did little to help her.

Mary had trouble forming relationships with men

because of her deep, undying anger. From her first serious relationship, she had a son, Luke. He gave her a reason to live, to survive, to fend off those nagging notions of suicide.

Mary ended up living on welfare and checks from strangers who had been touched by her story. Aimlessly, Mary and her son moved from town to town, but she could never hold on to a steady job.

By 1988—ten years after that horrific night—she thought her life finally had turned around. She married a 23-year-old landscaper and gave birth to another son, Alan. But the joy of having a family was soon ripped apart by fear.

Larry Singleton, the barbaric rapist, was back on the streets a free man.

Given time off for good behavior, Singleton—who never showed a bit of remorse—was unconditionally released because prison officials claimed he had been cured of alcoholism and was "completely, absolutely defused as a threat to society."

Mary was terrified. The stress of knowing he was out there, somewhere, waiting to finish the job as he had threatened in court, filled her with such dread she couldn't function. She felt faint every time there was a knock on the door. She couldn't look strangers in the face. Her emotional turmoil was too much for her marriage to bear, and it fell apart within three years of Singleton's release. After her divorce, she barely ate and her body dwindled to a skeletal 98 pounds.

With no money, no husband, no prospects, and no hope, she moved her two young sons into an abandoned, unheated garage in a small town near Tacoma, Washington. Although she lacked most everything, including self-confidence and self-esteem, Mary somehow managed to keep her little family together. If she was nothing else, she knew she was a survivor.

Meanwhile, there was such a public outcry over Singleton's release that he was hounded out of every California town in which he tried to live. He moved to Florida, where he kept a low profile until the spring of 1997, when a neighbor called police and reported seeing the 69-year-old Singleton strangling a nude woman in his house.

When police arrived, they found Singleton drunk with his shirt open and blood smeared over his chest. "I cut myself chopping vegetables," he slurred to the officers. Inside cops found the nude, bloody corpse of a 31-year-old prostitute; she had been stabbed seven times in the face and chest. Months later, Singleton was convicted of murder.

Despite her fears and the misery of her life, Mary flew to Tampa to testify during the sentencing phase of Singleton's murder trial. "Do you see your attacker in the courtroom?" the judge asked her.

"Yes," she said, as she raised one of her metal hooks and pointed it at Singleton. She boldly looked him straight in the eye, then told the court of Singleton's heinous 1978 attack and the physical and emotional toll it had taken. The judge sentenced Singleton to death. (Three years later he died of cancer while still on death row.)

Having helped put Singleton away for good, Mary gained back her health and self-confidence. In 1998, with a new outlook on life, she moved to Orange County in Southern California and got a reasonably priced apartment and her first decent job as a clerk in the district attorney's office. There, she met Tom Wilson, a 52-year-old investigator, and fell in love with him. They were married in March 1999.

With a new husband to support her, Mary began coming out of her shell and founded the Mary Vincent Foundation to help victims of violent crimes. Her fight for survival finally had found a purpose. "I lost twenty years of my life," she said. "I'm not going to lose another twenty. I'm going to do everything I can to make a difference in life."

THE SIERRA SURVIVOR

Mr. and Mrs. Harold Steeves's hearts sank when they heard the grim news on May 9, 1957. Their 23-year-old son, Air Force lieutenant David A. Steeves, and his jet had disappeared somewhere over California's rugged Sierra Mountains and he was now considered missing. The couple began to pray and hope.

After two anxiety-ridden weeks, during which 191 search missions combed the area without discovering a hint of the whereabouts of the pilot or the wreckage of the plane, the couple received word that the Air Force had called off the hunt for their son. Although disconsolate, his parents refused to give up hope.

Days later, right before Mother's Day, the telegram that every serviceman's parent fears arrived at the Steeveses' home in Trumbull, Connecticut. In it, the

Air Force informed the couple that their son's status had been changed. No longer was he considered missing. Now he was declared dead.

Still the couple clung to hope. David was strong, athletic, and resourceful. Why, hadn't he hitchhiked from California to Alaska by himself when he was only 17? And hadn't he always remained calm in difficult situations? They just couldn't believe he was gone, although the strength of their conviction was weakening.

Then on May 28, the day before Memorial Day, they received an official Air Force letter telling them it was hopeless to think that their son could have survived in that wild terrain. The Steeveses knew they couldn't deny the bleak facts much longer.

Finally, right before Flag Day, the death certificate of their son arrived in the mail. Only then did the couple accept that their strapping, handsome, blue-eyed boy was officially dead.

But they were dead wrong.

At that moment, their son was waging a dire struggle for survival alone in the untamed, harsh wilderness.

First Lieutenant David Steeves's adversity began when he took off in his two-seat Lockheed T-33 jet trainer from Hamilton Air Force Base, near San Francisco, for a flight to Craig Air Force Base, near Selma, Alabama. As he reached 33,000 feet, he radioed his position and settled back for what he thought would be smooth flying to his home base.

About 75 miles east of Fresno, California, he suddenly found himself fighting for his life.

Steeves heard a loud crackling sound in the cockpit and then a deafening, explosive boom that momentarily knocked him out cold. When he regained consciousness, he faced a scene of horror. Fire was ravaging the cockpit, singeing his face and devouring the controls. His helmet was melting in the heat as smoke consumed the cockpit, stinging his eyes and throat. Blood was trickling down the back of his neck.

Trying to keep his cool, Steeves feverishly worked the controls, but it was a futile effort. The plane refused to respond. As the cockpit continued to burn and fill with swirling, dense smoke, the jet began lurching from side to side and was losing altitude.

I'm going down! he thought. *Time to bail out—now!*

There was no time to send out a "Mayday," no time to send up a prayer. Blindly, he fell back on the skills he had honed during his cadet training and two years in the service. He activated his ejection seat and blasted out of the fiery jet as it continued its erratic flight.

His parachute billowed open, yanking him sharply, then dropping him with unusual speed in a spinning spiral toward earth. *Why am I falling so fast?* he wondered. He looked up to see rips in two panels of the light fabric. Glancing down, he saw he was over a vast primitive wilderness of formidable snow-capped granite peaks.

With limited control of his parachute, he whizzed by snowy slopes and headed for the only rock out-cropping that was void of snow. *I'm coming in too fast,* he thought. *Stay loose, don't tense up. This is it.*

Steeves slammed into the rock so hard he knocked himself out. After regaining consciousness hours later, he tried to stand. But the pain around his ankles was too great and he slumped to the ground. Dazed, he tried to get up again but faltered. After loosening his boots, Steeves put his hands around his ankles and found that they were red and swollen. The jarring landing had badly sprained them and, he would later learn, had torn several ligaments. He loosened the laces of his boots and started to take them off but then stopped. *I might not get them on again,* he said to himself.

He then checked his body for other injuries. He had sustained several bumps and bruises and a nasty laceration on the back of his head, but other-wise he was okay—except, of course, for his ankles.

He felt his pockets, knowing that whatever was in them now was his survival gear. When the plane exploded, he had bailed out so quickly that he hadn't had time to grab a survival kit. In one pocket he found his pipe, some loose wooden matches, and a half-used matchbook. "No tobacco," he muttered with a bitter smile.

From another pocket he pulled out his identification papers, some cash, and two photographs. One was of his pretty 21-year-old wife, Rita, in her wedding dress; the other was of his 15-month-old daughter, Leisa. He smiled and tucked them gently back in his pocket.

The only other things he had were a fountain pen, a mechanical pencil, and the .32-caliber revolver that he carried in an ankle holster.

"Oh, great," he lamented. "Not even a chocolate bar or anything to eat."

He shivered and hugged the parachute tightly around himself but he was still freezing. His clothing wasn't much help. He was wearing thin, warm-weather overalls that would have been fine if things had gone as planned and he had landed in Alabama. But they wouldn't help much in the wintry, wind-whipped Sierra Nevada Mountains.

He had fallen onto a rocky depression at about 11,000 feet, just above the timberline in a desolate area near Lake Helen in Kings Canyon National Park. Up above him, 12,000-foot-high snow-lined ridges ringed backcountry that even the hardiest, best-equipped hikers wouldn't tackle except in the brief summer months.

Steeves, who had never gone camping in his life, was poorly prepared to endure the rigors of such frozen heights at a time of year when much of the region was impassable. But the downed pilot did have several traits in his favor. He possessed a hardy physique (six feet tall, 195 pounds), ingenuity, faith, and a will to live. And he also was wearing a new pair of high lace-up combat boots.

But with no food and no water around him, there was no hope unless he got off the large snowless outcropping. *I've got to start walking down the mountain,* he told himself. With the parachute wrapped firmly around him to ward off the chilly wind, he slowly stood up and took one step. He nearly fainted from the pain. *There's no way I'm going to make it. But if I stay here, I'll die.*

For more than an hour he sat despondently on the cold rock. Then he pulled out the photos of Rita and Leisa. *I've got to get up. I've got to keep moving.* He tried to do so repeatedly, but each time he tumbled to the ground after just a step or two. "Keep moving!" he shouted to himself.

Realizing that he was in no condition to stand up and walk, he began crawling on his hands and knees. *This is weird,* he thought. *Here I am crawling on the ground while little Leisa is walking all over*

the house. I wonder what she's doing right now. I wonder if the Air Force has told Rita that I'm dead.

At times when the rock was steep, Steeves found it easier to roll. Sometimes he took a long rest, then painfully rose and walked a few steps before falling again. After a whole day of this agonizing progress, he had traveled only about a quarter of a mile. But it was enough to reach a lifeline—a patch of snow that he could melt in his mouth for water.

Nearby was a stand of trees where, on his hands and knees, he gathered twigs and dead branches. *I've got wood and matches so I'll build a fire to stay warm. Hopefully someone will see the smoke and find me. God, I hope they haven't given up on me.* His chest heaving with excitement, he rested against a boulder and tried to light his bundle of sticks. But after several attempts nothing caught. *The wood is too wet. I could sit here and strike every match I have and it'll never catch.*

A nippy wind swept down as the sun dipped behind the ridge. Steeves pulled the parachute tautly around him and crawled to the lee side of the boulder, where he spent his first night in the wilderness. When morning came, he knew staying there meant death, so he pushed onward. During the succeeding days he crawled and at night he huddled behind a boulder.

On the fourth night he burrowed into a rotted

hollow log to sleep. Although he felt weak from hunger, Steeves was encouraged the next day because the swelling in his ankles had started to go down, allowing him to walk gingerly. The going was slow, about a mile a day.

For the next week he sometimes had to roll down steep embankments, claw his way over fields of jagged ice-covered rocks, and slide on cold mud. Although he was shivering, he dumped his parachute because it was becoming a drag to wear.

For 12 days, he had nothing but snow water to sustain him. Not a single morsel of food crossed his lips. Famished and fatigued, Steeves was losing hope that he could survive much longer. *Oh,* he thought, *what I wouldn't give for a peanut butter and jelly sandwich.*

Then he came upon a green meadow. He stopped in amazement and rubbed his eyes at the blessed sight in front of him. There stood a tiny log cabin. Thoughts of food, supplies, and warmth whirled around in his head. Although each footfall sent pain through his body, he loped to the door and knocked. There was no answer. After peering through the windows and seeing it was unoccupied, he broke the glass and climbed inside.

The place was a forest ranger's structure filled with tools and equipment for measuring and clearing snow. Everything inside was neatly arranged and cared for, although it seemed the cabin hadn't been used in many months.

Steeves rushed to a cabinet and flung open the doors. "Yes! Yes! Yes!" he shouted gleefully, looking at shelves displaying a treasure trove of cans of beans and ham and other staples, packets of soup flakes and sugar. "Food!" Rather than wait to collect kindling and start a fire, he ravenously feasted on beans and ham, the first meal to soothe his empty, shrunken stomach in almost two weeks.

After he gobbled his food, he decided to make a fire, but the wood he gathered wouldn't light. So he used the papers in his pocket. *I've got money to burn,* he thought as he held a match to several dollar bills. Next went his ID, but not the pictures in his wallet.

He found a map of the area and figured out that he was in Simpson Meadow. Stashed in a corner of the cabin were magazines, books, and records of campers. Over the next two weeks, he used them to make fires, but only after he read them first. Unfortunately, in all the publications, large sections of pages were torn out so he never got to read a complete magazine. However, he read one intact article offering tips on how to survive in the Arctic. But he no longer needed the information. He was down under the frost line, at 6,000 feet, where the days were getting warmer as June approached.

The only book containing all its pages was a

cookbook, which was a blessing and a curse. Thumbing through it made his mouth water and he dreamed of a banquet of sumptuous food, but it also made him yearn for the wonderful meals Rita made for him. The pages in the cookbook were among the last sacrificed to make his fires.

He spared a few sheets of paper on which he scribbled notes about his ordeal from the time he bailed out until he arrived at the cabin. *If they find me dead, at least they'll know what happened to me,* he thought.

But he didn't plan on dying. Although not a religious person, he began to talk to God and gain faith that he would survive. After all, what were the odds that in this vast wilderness he would stumble upon this cabin? He was beginning to believe a higher power had guided him there.

By the tenth day at the cabin, much of his strength had returned and his ankles continued to heal. But he also had polished off most of the canned food, so he knew he needed to find new food sources.

To his joy, he discovered some fishing line and a couple of rusty hooks that he had overlooked earlier. Steeves hobbled out to the banks of a tributary of the Kings River, dug some grubs out of a tree for bait, tossed in the line, and enjoyed fresh trout that evening. A couple of days later, he decided to try for bigger game. Although his sore ankles prevented him from tracking a deer, he devised an ingenious trap. He tied his revolver to a sapling next to a salt lick and rigged a trip wire. A couple of nights later in the dead of night he heard the unmistakable.

An animal obviously had tripped the wire, firing the gun. Steeves wanted to check it out, but the darkness kept him inside the cabin. At first light, he hobbled toward the salt lick and let out a triumphant shout when he saw from a distance that he had dropped a deer. *Fresh venison tonight!* he thought. *I'll have enough meat for days!*

But his joy was tempered when he reached the dead deer. Mountain lions had beaten him to the prize, which was already half eaten. Using a knife he found in the cabin, he cut off what he could, then cooked it.

It was gone within a few days, but by then he discovered new sources of food, including green snakes. Wild strawberries and dandelions were sprouting as temperatures warmed up and spring showers melted the snow higher up on the mountain.

About a month after he had bailed out of his stricken jet, Steeves felt he was strong enough to hike out. He spread out the park map and charted a course that would take him to a little stream, a minor tributary of the Kings River. He would wade across it and head to a road that, according to the map, would lead him to civilization.

After walking several miles through deep gorges, he came to what was supposed to be the placid little brook. To his dismay, he discovered it was a raging river swollen by snow melt and several recent cloudbursts. *I have no choice,* he thought. *I have to chance it.* He stepped into the frigid rushing water, trying to feel his way along the rocky bottom. Suddenly he slipped, fell and was pulled under. He surfaced, gasping for air, but the powerful torrent swept him under again. Thrashing wildly as he slammed against the rocks, he grabbed hold of a fallen tree and lifted himself out of the water and onto a muddy bank.

He was shivering and catching his breath when he thought, *The pictures! Oh, God, I hope I didn't lose them.* He dug his hand into his pocket and pulled out the photos of Rita and Leisa. They were wet but still intact. With a deep sigh of relief, he picked himself up and headed back to the cabin. Five days later, after another unsuccessful try at the river, he abandoned his idea to reach the other side and returned to the cabin to figure out another game plan. The two attempts had sapped his strength, so he stayed at the cabin for another three weeks eating trout and wild greens and dreaming of returning to his family.

In the six weeks since the accident, his usually clean-shaven face had become covered with a thick, grizzled, reddish beard. *What will Rita think of my*

The Sierra Survivor

new look if she ever gets to see me again? It was especially distressing to him when June 23 came and went. He had spent his second wedding anniversary away from his beloved wife.

Missing out on his anniversary strengthened his resolve to get out. *There doesn't seem to be an easy way down from here. How do people get into here?* He stared at the map until he figured a new way out—a mountain pass several miles away that led to a valley called Granite Basin and a road to a ranger station. *Of course! Instead of going down, I have to go up and over.* To get to Granite Basin, he had to climb up the 10,600-foot Granite Pass and then hike down, a total distance of 12 grueling miles.

Steeves set out early Sunday morning, June 30. The going was rough and slow and his ankles ached with each step, but he kept a steady pace. By the time he had hiked through the pass and was heading down toward Granite Basin, dusk was settling in. He was looking for a spot to spend the night when he saw a light flickering a few hundred yards ahead. *Is it what I think it is?* he wondered. His heart pounding in anticipation, he plodded on until he broke through a thick stand of pines. *Yes! It's a campfire!*

Two wilderness lovers, Albert Ade of Squaw Valley and Dr. Charles Howard, a dentist from Fresno, had pitched a tent and were sitting around their campfire when they were startled by a tall, gaunt, bearded figure emerging from the darkness. For the first time since he fell out of the sky 53 days earlier, Steeves finally had made human contact.

After telling them of his astounding odyssey, Steeves was treated by the campers to a dinner of steak grilled over the open fire. As much as he wanted to get to the ranger station, Steeves was dog-tired and fell into a deep, contented sleep. *I made it,* he told himself before nodding off. *I'm going to survive.*

The following morning Steeves arrived at the Cedar Grove Ranger Station, riding on Dr. Howard's horse and guided by Ade. Forest rangers estimated Steeves had walked about 30 miles through brutal terrain. Even men as experienced as the rangers were amazed that he survived. Although he had lost 30 pounds, he was in good condition.

The first thing he did was phone home. He tried Rita, but no one answered. So he had the operator dial his mother. "Would you accept a collect call from Lieutenant David Arthur Steeves?" the operator asked.

On the line, Steeves heard his mother gasp. "I most certainly will," she said somewhat hesitatingly because she wasn't sure if this was a sick joke. But when she heard his voice, she knew that her prayers had been answered. Her son David had come back from the dead.

The Sierra Survivor

When Rita was given the fantastic news she went into shock because she had already accepted his death. After she had been informed officially on May 28 that she was a widow, she immediately had sold their mobile home in Selma, Alabama, stored their furniture, and enrolled at Bridgeport University in Connecticut with plans to become a teacher.

Meanwhile, reporters flocked to the young flier with the movie star looks, wanting to know how he survived. "At the beginning, I didn't know if I was going to make it," he told them. "As time went on I began to develop faith. I'd never been a very religious man, but this faith in God grew stronger and stronger. That, plus love for my wife and child drove me."

A few days later, Steeves flew east to be reunited with his loved ones. At the emotional reunion, Rita took one look at his beard, which he had not touched since his ordeal ended, and joked, "Dave, you look horrible!"

Horrible or not, David Steeves became an overnight sensation. He accepted offers to appear on TV with the biggest names of the era—Arthur Godfrey, Dave Garroway, Art Linkletter, and Ed Sullivan. He went on a game show and received $1,250 from an electric shaver manufacturer for shaving off his beard in front of the cameras. He signed a book contract with Henry Holt & Co. and a $10,000 deal for his story with the *Saturday Evening Post*.

But as difficult as it was to survive in the wild, Steeves faced another test of survival—the survival of his good name.

When not a single piece of wreckage from his T-33 could be found, the cheering stopped. Rumor and innuendo surrounded him, fueled, in part, by Americans' Cold War fears that Communists were infiltrating the country. He'd sold the plane to the Russians. He'd shipped the jet piecemeal to Mexico. He'd concocted his story to make money off it. He was a traitor, a liar, a con man. It was all a hoax.

Steeves insisted that his tale of survival was true. "I told the story as it happened. They can't disprove my story," he told the press. "How can they? Are they going to interview the animals?"

As doubts mounted, his life went into a tailspin. The Air Force became suspicious and launched an inquiry. They grilled Steeves for hours and forced him to undergo psychiatric examinations. He asked for, and was granted, a discharge, which ended his dream of making a career in the Air Force.

Abruptly, both his lucrative book and magazine deals were canceled. But the worst blow of all came when Rita filed for divorce and took their daughter with her.

His reputation all but ruined, Steeves moved to

The Sierra Survivor

Fresno, where he remarried, worked as a commercial pilot, and designed planes. Whenever he found extra money and time, he rented a plane and scoured the Sierras in search of the wreckage. But it was all in vain. His jet was either still hidden deep in the wilderness or it somehow had flown on its own before crashing into the Pacific Ocean.

In 1963, the breach of contract suits that he had filed five years earlier against the book publisher and magazine were settled out of court. But that did little to clear his name. He knew the only way to do that was to find the wreckage or even a small piece of it. Despite repeated efforts, he never found the proof he needed to back up his story.

In 1965 at the age of 31, Steeves was killed when the single-engine cargo plane he had modified crashed during takeoff in Boise, Idaho.

The strange case of the Sierra survivor was all but forgotten until 1977, twelve years after his death. Two Boy Scouts were hiking in Kings Canyon National Park in an extremely rugged area that few people had ever traversed when they came upon a large piece of Plexiglas. Rangers later recovered it and identified it as a cockpit canopy. It bore the serial number 52-92-32, the same serial number as the missing jet of Lieutenant David A. Steeves.

THE ATOMIC MAN

Harold "Mac" McCluskey knew that following orders from his superiors could be dangerous for him and the others working the midnight-to-eight shift at the U.S. Department of Energy's Hanford Nuclear Reservation in the state of Washington.

But he reluctantly did what he was told . . . and paid a terrible price.

An explosion sprayed him with radioactive debris, causing serious injuries and blasting him with a dose of radiation 500 times the maximum safe level for a human.

Yet despite being the most radioactive person in the world, Harold McCluskey survived.

Before he became a medical phenomenon, the 64-year-old technician was the head nuclear process operator at the Hanford plant. The plant originally had been built in 1944 to produce plutonium for atomic bombs but now was used primarily to recover radioactive byproducts from nuclear waste.

In the wee hours of August 30, 1976, McCluskey was supposed to extract hazardous americium-241, a plutonium byproduct used in minuscule amounts in smoke detectors. Fifty times more radioactive than plutonium, americium-241 was one of the most toxic man-made substances of its time. Tiny amounts had been shown to cause raging cancers in laboratory animals.

In the extraction process, highly concentrated nitric acid was sent through columns of resin to remove the americium. It was done in a heavy-gauge steel cabinet called a glove box that had double-thick leaded-glass windows and plastic glove ports so the operator could see inside and reach inside to adjust the valves.

On that fateful night, McCluskey, a technician with more than 25 years of experience, was uneasy. He believed conditions were ripe for a catastrophe.

Unfortunately, he was right.

Hanford workers had just returned from a five-month strike that had closed down the plant. During the long labor dispute, nothing in the plant had been touched, including the americium-soaked resin that had been loaded into the extraction columns before the walkout months earlier.

That's what worried McCluskey. In all his years

working at Hanford, he was told that these resins had to be fresh. *Start the extraction process using resin even three months old, and you could have one big explosion on your hands*, he thought. *This stuff has been sitting around for two months longer than that.*

McCluskey mentioned his concerns to his supervisor, who relayed the message to the top brass. The higher-ups ordered McCluskey to go ahead with the process.

For a moment, McCluskey considered storming out the door, but he thought better of it. He had been at Hanford most of his adult life and was on the brink of retiring. Besides, where could a 64-year-old guy with a high school education get another job that paid as well as this one? This was no time to walk away in a huff.

Despite his misgivings, McCluskey donned his protective equipment—thick coveralls, mask, and respirator—designed specifically for working near radioactive materials. Then he went to work at the glove ports.

All seemed to be going smoothly until around two A.M. At that point, work stopped and a sample of the processed material was drawn and sent off to the lab to be analyzed. But McCluskey's experienced eye didn't need a lab report to tell him that something was wrong. The sample was a dark orange, a color that suggested to him the resin had deteriorated during the strike and was no good.

As the lab looked at the sample, McCluskey and a fellow worker, Marvin Klundt, chatted until around 2:45 A.M. when they heard an odd hissing sound coming from the glove box. Through the thick glass, McCluskey saw curling brown steam. "Iodine fumes!" he hollered to Klundt. Just as the veteran technician feared, the resins were unstable and were breaking down while their vapors filled the glove box. McCluskey had seen this happen before, but never at such a rapid rate.

"Call for help!" McCluskey yelled to Klundt, who scurried off to the phone. Meanwhile, McCluskey shoved his hands into the glove ports so he could adjust the valves in an attempt to vent the glove box. His gloves felt warm, the hissing grew louder, and the vapors got thicker—all ominous signs. Within seconds, the clouds became so dense he couldn't see the gauges inside. Suddenly, a new, louder hissing noise erupted from the bottom of the column.

"The pressure's building up!" McCluskey shouted to Klundt. "This thing's going to blow!"

As he was about to turn and run, McCluskey spotted a partially opened door. He decided to close it so that any radioactive fumes from an explosion would not endanger workers on the other side. But before he had the chance, the glove box exploded in a blinding flash of blue light.

The blast blew out the double-thick windows and glove ports and knocked McCluskey, who was only five feet away, across the room. The force of the explosion ripped off his mask, and his face, neck, and shoulders were pelted with acid, resin, glass and metal shards—and radioactive americium.

Amid the swirling fumes, he gasped for air. But every breath he took filled his lungs with the deadly, toxic radioactive dust.

Blind and bleeding, he called out, "I can't see! I can't see! Help me!"

Although he didn't have a protective mask, Klundt ran back into the treacherous cloud of fumes, grabbed McCluskey and dragged him into the corridor 50 feet away.

While radiation sensors in the building wailed their warning, the plant's emergency medical team stripped McCluskey's torn, bloody radioactive clothes and put him in a decontamination tub. They kept talking to him, asking him questions, but he couldn't make much sense of what they were saying. It didn't matter, because all the chatter was simply to keep him from fainting as the medical team frantically worked to wash off the deadly particles.

Not only did he suffer acid burns to his face, but he also sustained serious eye damage. He couldn't see because his corneas were scorched and his eyelids were blistered. His ears also had been harmed by the blast so that voices sounded muffled to him.

He was rushed to the Emergency Decontamination Facility (EDF) in nearby Richland, where doctors and nurses wore special hoods, masks, coveralls, gloves, and shoe covers. When the ambulance arrived, McCluskey was put on a stretcher attached to a rail on the ceiling and guided to a room lined in lead. He was placed on a table surrounded by lead-filled steel sides and lead glass shields to protect the medical personnel from radiation. After nurses washed him with detergent soap and baby shampoo, doctors used forceps to painstakingly pluck out fine radioactive particles of glass, metal, and resin that were embedded in his skin.

In throbbing pain and lapsing in and out of consciousness, McCluskey was alert enough to overhear an unsettling conversation between eight doctors. Four of them speculated that his chances for immediate survival were, at best, fifty-fifty. The other four shook their heads, indicating their belief he was a doomed man.

By all standards, McCluskey appeared to be a lost cause. He had received, in a few brief seconds, the largest dose of americium-241 ever recorded—at least five hundred times greater than what scientists considered a safe exposure, and even that was cumulative over a lifetime. No human had ever been exposed to such a tremendous amount before, so doctors lacked experience dealing with this level of radiation. There was no medical textbook they could follow. They didn't know how McCluskey would react to the exposure or to the treatment or how long he would remain contaminated and a hazard to others—if he lived.

Most doctors were pretty sure of one thing. If he didn't die within days after the accident, it was almost certain he would die of cancer within the next few months or years. McCluskey knew the odds were stacked against him, and told the doctors, "I don't think I'm going to live very long." But that didn't mean he was giving up. Sustained by his deep Baptist faith, McCluskey bravely and stoically fought to survive. Although the doctors secretly agreed with his bleak self-assessment, they weren't giving up either and kept improvising in an unwavering effort to save him.

Their biggest problem was dealing with the radioactive particles coursing through his body—especially in his lungs, liver, and bones—which needed to be flushed out of his system. Although this was uncharted medical territory, the doctors decided to use injections of calcium DTPA, a chelating agent, meaning that it could chemically bind to the radioactive materials in McCluskey's blood so they could be excreted.

His doctors kept giving him intravenous injections of calcium DTPA until he had received more of the chemical than had ever been given to a human being. They soon discovered that their efforts to save him were beginning to kill him. Calcium DTPA did its job of flushing out the deadly radioactive metals. But it was also depleting him of zinc, an important element that the body needs to survive and heal. He faced possible intestinal and stomach bleeding as well as kidney problems.

Now the doctors wanted to gamble on another chelating agent, the experimental compound, zinc DTPA. But zinc DTPA had been tested only in animals. Nevertheless, the desperate doctors appealed to the Food and Drug Administration, which granted permission for McCluskey to be the first human guinea pig to receive the treatment.

In the beginning, McCluskey was only vaguely aware of what was happening. For the first two weeks, he couldn't see and he feared he would be blind for the rest of his life. But then one morning he opened his eyes and saw a glimmer of light. His sight began returning as the blinding acid burns to his corneas started to heal.

His colleague, Marvin Klundt, who had been slightly contaminated when he returned to pull

McCluskey to safety, was treated for nine days before returning to work.

Meanwhile, every day McCluskey had at least two baths, a full body shave, eye irrigations, and radiation scans. After the first three weeks, he was still too radioactive to be in the same room with an unprotected person. Geiger counters would start to chatter when they came within 50 feet of "the atomic man," as the media now called him.

For months he had to remain in isolation, living in a cement and lead room. His main human contacts were the nurses who gave him his daily scrubdowns and doctors who came to administer the zinc DTPA. He eventually received 600 shots of the chelation therapy, leaving his arm looking like knotty pine.

Although his injuries had healed after a couple of months, McCluskey couldn't go home until he was cleansed of contamination and posed no risk to others.

His wife, Ella, with whom he had celebrated 40 years of marriage the day before the accident, was allowed to visit him, but at first whispering sweet nothings was out of the question. She had to stay 30 feet away, covered head to toe in a space suit. Before she left she had to be checked with an alpha meter to make sure that no hot particles had stuck to her. McCluskey communicated with the outside world through a telephone near his bed dubbed "Harold's hotline."

He had to live in this weird isolation until Geiger counters were calm in his presence and there was no measurable americium on his breath. Even after repeated hard scrubbings of his skin, some residue still was left, so he had to remain in relative isolation until at least one layer of skin had been sloughed off. While waiting months before he could go home, he stayed in shape by riding an exercise bike and stayed calm by practicing his faith.

Slowly, steadily the radiation levels went down. Despite the poor odds, McCluskey continued to recover, much to the surprise of his doctors, who kept looking for anything that might hint of a "radiation effect." But the physical symptoms they expected—hair loss, lung problems, the destruction of bone marrow, and other signs of radiation sickness—didn't materialize.

McCluskey, whose face was scarred from acid burns, remained in isolation for five and a half months. He finally came home to Prosser, Washington, on Valentine's Day, 1977. "That's the longest graveyard shift I ever worked," he quipped.

But the ordeal was not over. He received regular medical treatment for years and had to carry a special container with him for his urine and feces because they had to be disposed of as radioactive wastes.

The Atomic Man

After his return home, he endured cataract surgery and a cornea replacement, kidney infections, four heart attacks, and a drop in the level of blood platelets, all related to the accident or the treatments. And although he was deemed to be no longer a risk to anyone, he was still radioactive, able to set off a Geiger counter when he held it to his face.

More troubling was the reaction of the citizens of Prosser. Many people, even old friends, were afraid of "the atomic man," fearful that they would be contaminated by him. Friends would call and talk to him, but they would decline invitations to visit his house or get together. Shop owners feared a loss of business if McCluskey was seen around their establishment too much. Out of courtesy, he rotated barbers so his presence wouldn't scare away customers.

Physically weakened by his ordeal, McCluskey sued the government, and eventually settled for $275,000 plus medical expenses. After that, he spent much of his time listening to Bible readings on audiotape and tending to his rose garden. Television was out of the question because it was too hard on his damaged eyes, which had become highly sensitive to light. The accident left him with too little strength to do much else except survive.

Months turned into years, and McCluskey quietly continued to defy the odds, crediting his staying power to "good care and our Creator." By all standards, he was a medical miracle.

When he died in 1987 at the age of 75, 11 years after the accident, it was from heart disease, not from radiation-induced cancer, which was what many thought would swiftly take the life of "the atomic man."

AGONY IN THE AMAZON

Lansa Airlines Flight 508 departed Lima, Peru, on Christmas Eve, 1971. It was carrying 92 people to the small town of Pucallpa, about 475 miles away in the Amazon jungle.

Among the passengers was pretty 17-year-old Juliane Koepcke, a petite, blue-eyed blonde who was wearing a cute new minidress and white high heels. She had just graduated from high school with honors and would soon be attending a university in West Germany to pursue her dream of studying zoology.

The teen was flying with her mother, Marie, a prominent ornithologist at the Lima Museum, to Pucallpa, where they would spend Christmas with Juliane's father, Hans, a zoologist who was conducting research in the jungle. Juliane had spent many vacations at the family's remote hut, where she and her parents studied the Amazon wildlife.

The Greatest Survivor Stories Never Told

The plane, a Lockheed Electra turbo prop, took off for the 90-minute flight in clear, sunny skies. It climbed above the snowy peaks of the Andes and was heading over the green canopy of the Amazon. Everyone was in a festive mood, especially Juliane, who was sitting in the third row from the back, next to the window. Her mother sat beside her and talked happily about their holiday plans.

But their flight to Pucallpa was about to turn into a flight into pandemonium.

Halfway to their destination, the skies suddenly darkened, angry clouds spewed rain and lightning, and the plane started shaking so violently that carry-on luggage began falling from the overhead bins.

Then Juliane heard a scream, and looked out the window at a terrifying sight. A bolt of lightning slammed into the right wing. Seconds later, the wing was consumed by fire.

"This is the end of everything!" her mother shrieked as a loud bang reverberated through the cabin. Before Juliane could gather her thoughts, the fuselage split open with a sickening crack, spilling passengers, seats, and luggage into the raging storm.

In horror, the girl found herself tumbling outside the plane, feeling so helpless and scared that she was too numb to even scream. Still strapped in her seat, Juliane somersaulted toward the jungle below.

Agony in the Amazon

Her last thought, before everything went black, was that the trees below looked like cauliflowers.

When she woke up hours later in a light rain, she was still strapped in her overturned seat, which was lying on the jungle floor next to two other seats. These seats, including the one where her mother had been, were empty. Juliane unbuckled her seat belt and crawled out from under the seat. She winced from a pain in her right shoulder—she later learned she had fractured her collarbone—and from several cuts and bruises to her arms and legs and a gash on her foot. One eye was swollen shut, but otherwise she seemed unhurt. As she tentatively stood up, she called out, "Anyone here?" but there was no answer.

Juliane looked at her watch, which amazingly was still keeping time. It was 4 P.M., about three hours since the plane had broken apart. As she glanced around the jungle, which was littered with seats, smashed luggage, and parts of the plane, she spotted only two bodies. "Hello! Hello! Is anybody out there?" she hollered. But there were no signs of any survivors.

Too exhausted to search the area, Juliane crawled back under the row of seats and curled up into a fetal position. She was encompassed by an eerie silence broken only by the rain and the persistent croaking of tree frogs and the chirping of jungle birds.

When morning came, she hurt from head to toe because the shock from her ordeal had worn off. She called out to any other possible survivors but she heard no response. She kept hoping that since she had survived the crash, maybe her mother had too. *I've got to try to find her,* she thought.

Juliane had trouble seeing and walking because she had lost her glasses and one shoe in the crash. She picked up a long stick and pounded the ground with it as she walked, a necessity in the jungle where, as she knew, poisonous snakes and spiders seemed to lurk at every step. Then she searched for her mother and possible survivors. Each step was agony for her as she slowly poked through the wreckage. She came upon a package lying in a pile of debris. Inside was a Christmas cake and some hard candies. The cake was drenched from the rain, but she took a bite out of it anyway. It tasted awful, so she threw it away, but she tucked the candies in her pocket.

Her search effort proved fruitless. *People are probably scattered all over for miles and miles,* she thought. She flinched at the mental images from the day before of her fellow passengers tumbling out of the splitting plane. *I can't stay here. Search planes aren't going to spot me in this thick jungle. I have to get out of here and find help.*

In the distance she heard the sound of a brook. Remembering the survival lessons her parents had

Agony in the Amazon

drilled into her during their years in the jungle, she figured her only hope for staying alive was to find and follow the water. Her parents repeatedly had told her that if she was ever lost in the jungle, she must look for running water. Small streams lead to rivers, which are the highways for the hunters and Indians of the jungle, the only humans who inhabited the area.

Following the running water, Juliane clambered over rocks and fallen trees and headed down a gorge. Soon the brook grew wider and was running faster. She was careful to stay on the banks as much as she could, even though thick, thorny vines covered the river's edge. They ripped at her feet and arms and tore her dress. But she stayed out of the river. She knew the waters were dangerous, filled with razor-toothed piranhas that could strip the flesh right off her.

Somewhere along the route, she lost her one remaining shoe in the muck, so she kept plodding on barefoot. The air was thick with huge, stinging, bloodthirsty mosquitoes and weird flying insects that can only thrive in the jungle.

At one point she heard the loud buzzing of flies. She followed the sound to another piece of the wreckage—an overturned row of seats. She knelt down beside them and then recoiled in disgust and horror. Three passengers—teenage girls like her—were still strapped into their seats. All were dead and all were covered with those disgusting buzzing insects.

She screamed and wept, and then she trudged on. She walked for three days. One time she heard vultures and found another piece of the plane, but she found no more passengers, alive or dead. From time to time she heard the sound of helicopters or airplanes overhead, no doubt searching for the downed airliner. She yelled for help, even though she knew it was in vain. They were too high to hear a small voice crying in a jungle too thick for them to see into.

The solitary survivor continued to follow the stream. She was thankful she had fresh water to drink, but she was famished. Her only food consisted of a few pieces of hard candy in her pocket. She considered eating some of the fat toads she spotted, but she was afraid they might be poisonous.

Four days passed and, as she had hoped, the stream turned into a river.

However, she was running out of time. The gash on her foot and smaller cuts on her arms had turned into festering wounds. Attracted to the infections, flies had landed in the gashes and laid eggs, which had hatched out into hundreds of squirming maggots. Juliane tried to dig them out, but there were too many. She tried to blot out of her mind that worms were eating her alive.

Having finished all the candy, Juliane was

starved, but she didn't want to touch the jungle fruit because she couldn't tell the difference between those that were good and the ones that were poisonous. At least she had all the fresh water she could drink.

At night, she curled up at the side of the river and tried to sleep, despite the swarms of mosquitoes that attacked her and the large jungle animals that scared her by creeping along the bank or slithering into the water nearby. Her only hope was to keep moving, so each day she pressed on. The 100°-plus heat, hunger, and her injuries were robbing her of strength with every passing minute, but still she kept trekking. Nearly swooning from the heat and humidity, she gave in to the temptation to swim and wade in the river, praying that the piranhas would leave her alone.

Most of the time Juliane walked or crawled, picking her way carefully along the river bank, clawing over logs and massive boulders. It was slow going. She had to watch where she put her feet because of the poisonous snakes, crabs, and thorns. Broad armies of ants on the march often blocked her path, forcing her to take detours. Despite the threat of piranhas, she often swam in the river because the current carried her much faster than she could walk. But eventually the water was rushing too swiftly for her to swim at all. She trudged on slowly, painfully, trusting that at any moment she would stumble onto civilization. But day after day, her anticipation at finding another human was never fulfilled.

Finally, nine days after the crash, the swollen, pain-wracked teenager stumbled onto a small beach and thought her prayers had been answered. To her joy, she spotted a sign of human life—a canoe. It looked new. Behind it she saw a path through dense foliage which led to a hut. *Help at last!* she thought.

Juliane hobbled to the hut and carefully pushed open the door. Inside she found a carefully wrapped outboard motor. But there were no people, no food, no signs that anyone had been there for weeks. Her heart sank. The hut was probably a lean-to for hunters, and it could be weeks, or even months, before they returned. By then it would be too late.

She had had nothing but river water in her stomach for days and was ravenous. But an even bigger concern were the worms that had burrowed into her skin and were eating her flesh. With a piece of palm wood the young woman pulled dozens of the wriggling maggots out of her skin. *God, help me!* she thought. *They're eating me alive. If I ever do make it out of here, they'll probably have to amputate my arms and feet.* But she was too tired to feel sorry for herself. She curled up on the hard floor and went to sleep. At least she was dry for the first time in days.

Juliane woke up to a heavy downpour the next

Agony in the Amazon

morning, but nevertheless she figured she should leave the safety of her shelter and move on. *Chances are slim that anyone will come and find me,* she thought. She considered taking the canoe and attempting to paddle downstream. But her strict upbringing kept her from doing it. After all, it wasn't hers and she didn't want to steal it. Besides, she felt too weak to handle the strong current.

Back in the hut, the dying girl listened to the sound of the rain and the screeches of monkeys and parrots. Then she thought she heard a new sound, a wonderful sound—human voices.

Moments later, three hunters, dripping wet from the rain, burst into the hut. "What have we here?" said one of the astonished men, speaking Spanish.

Juliane tearfully told her story of struggle and survival. They knelt beside her, offering her the only food they had, sugar, salt, and flour flavored with cassava. "Eat, eat, eat," one said.

Although she was hungry, she couldn't eat. She was so desperate to get rid of the squirming maggots in her skin that she could think of nothing else. She begged them to help her. Some time ago, she had seen her father use petrol to draw worms out of the skin of her pet dog, so she had the men pour gasoline over her wounds. At least 35 worms wriggled their way out of her arms. Then the men put salve on her wounds, and made a fruit mash for her, but still she refused to eat. She wanted to move on, but it was already dark, and the hunters said it would be foolhardy to attempt the river at night.

They gently covered her with blankets and mosquito netting, and then they talked for hours. One of the men had been in the search planes looking for the wreckage of Flight 508, but they had seen nothing from the air.

In the morning, the men helped Juliane into the canoe and paddled for a couple of hours to the hut of an Indian woman who they said could help her. *Finally, I'll get some medical care,* Juliane thought. But after one look at the scratched-up blonde, whose face was swollen and whose eyes were so bloodshot they were red slits, the woman shrieked, "Demon!" She shooed Juliane and the men away.

The hunters paddled on in the treacherous rain-swollen river. Nearly eight hours later, they reached the town of Tournavista, where a doctor treated Juliane's wounds. From there, an American pilot, Jerrie Cobb, flew her to a missionary camp near Pucallpa where her father was waiting for her.

The rains delayed a 12-man foot patrol from immediately reaching the site of the crash, but they eventually found the wreckage, scattered over 10 miles of jungle. They confirmed that Juliane was the only person to live through the nightmare. The other 91 passengers, including her mother, had perished.

Agony in the Amazon

Searchers said that they found evidence that about a dozen other passengers had survived the crash and clung to life for days before dying from untreated injuries. Had Juliane waited for help, had the rains been heavier, had the hunters come a few days later, she surely would have ended up among the dead, too. As one member of the search party put it, "Only God knows how that girl survived."

To Juliane, the question was more basic: "Why was I spared?"

THE CHAMBER OF DREAD

There was nothing unusual about the summer morning of August 4, 1993—it was just your typical work-a-day Thursday at the Mark Twain Diner on Northern Boulevard in Jackson Heights, New York. The cook, Spiro Pavlatos, was frying eggs in the kitchen and Corrine Perez, the waitress, was pouring a refill of black coffee for one of her regulars, 68-year-old Harvey Weinstein.

For five years, Weinstein had followed the same routine. Around seven A.M. every weekday he parked his gray Saab out front, then planted himself on one of the Naugahyde seats and ordered the same breakfast: cranberry juice, raisin bran, rye toast, and black coffee. Then, while reading the sports pages, he smoked three Marlboro Lights. Before leaving for work at the Lord West Formal Wear factory 15 blocks away, he would receive a lecture from Corrine, who had become his good friend over the years, about his chain-smoking habit. "You should quit," she always said. "They're no good for you."

To all appearances Weinstein was just another unassuming working guy, but appearances in this case were deceiving. The trim, methodical gentleman with the full head of salt-and-pepper hair who ate his raisin bran every morning at the formica counter didn't just work at the Lord West factory; he owned it.

Weinstein was known as New York's "tuxedo king." His company was the second-largest formal wear manufacturer in the country and he was worth millions. Everyone in the diner knew it, but no one gave it a second thought. To the cooks, waitresses, countermen, and other patrons at the Mark Twain, Weinstein was just another one of the regulars.

On this day, Weinstein paid up, said goodbye, and headed toward his car. But this morning would be different. This morning would be the beginning of a journey into a hellhole for Harvey Weinstein.

As he reached for the door of his car, at around 7:45 A.M., a man came from behind, grabbed him by the shoulders, and put a knife to his throat.

"Get in the car, quietly," ordered the assailant in a heavy Spanish accent. Then the knife wielder and two accomplices shoved Weinstein into the front passenger seat. From the back seat, one the abductors placed a metal wire noose around the victim's neck and slapped a blindfold over his eyes. Then the car roared off. The abduction had taken no more than 20 seconds.

"This is a kidnapping," Weinstein was told. "The ransom is five million."

"You'd better kill me now," Weinstein replied. He might be the wealthy tuxedo king, but he wasn't that rich. In his mind he tallied the available cash in his bank accounts and knew he was going to be plenty short. *Maybe they've kidnapped the wrong guy,* he thought. *Maybe they were aiming for that other Harvey Weinstein, the megabucks movie mogul.*

"I think you've made a mistake," said Weinstein. "You've got the wrong guy."

"Shut up!" his kidnappers snapped.

They drove for about a half an hour to a wooded area where they stopped and marched Weinstein several yards before shoving him into a pit about eight feet deep. With metal bands they shackled his legs, his right arm, and his waist to what he assumed was a steal beam against the wall.

They left him there half lying, half crouching and covered the muddy, dank hole with a large, heavy steel slab. The last thing he heard, before his captors disappeared, was the rustling of leaves and branches over the cover, a final touch of camouflage. All was quiet except for the sounds of cars speeding along a highway nearby during the morning rush hour.

Weinstein managed to remove the blindfold, but it didn't matter. No light filtered down from above. When he held his hand in front of his face, he saw nothing; it was pitch black. *This*, he thought, *must be what it's like to be blind.*

After a while Weinstein pulled free from the metal bands that strapped him to the beam. When he moved around, he realized how small the chamber was—about five feet by five feet.

His captors had left him a blanket to sleep on, but his cell was too tiny for him to lie down. He could rest only with his feet or his back up against the wall. He felt around the walls of his prison and found a ledge at eye level and a rock. He used the rock as a chair. The hellhole was insulated with sheets of plastic bubble wrap. Several three-inch tubes that ran out the top of the hole dangled several feet over Weinstein's head and provided his only air supply. A hundred-pound steel plate, pushed over the top and further weighted down by three wooden planks and two cinder blocks, assured the abductors that even if he broke from his shackles he wouldn't be able to escape. The entire grave was obscured from view by six inches of brush and dirt.

Weinstein waited alone in total darkness, trying desperately not to panic, trying hard to stay calm.

The Chamber of Dread

Still, he wondered whether he would ever again see his family, friends, the Lord West factory, the Mark Twain Diner, or daylight.

Aboveground a lot of people were wondering too—wondering and worrying. Weinstein had promised to pick up his daughter at 9:00 A.M. at LaGuardia Airport, but he had failed to show up. Two hours later, he missed a meeting at Lord West. This was so unlike the caring father and the buttoned-down businessman that everyone knew right away that something was very, very wrong. His daughter called the police and reported him missing. His Saab was found later that day abandoned in Brooklyn.

Nothing happened until the next morning, when the president of Lord West, Ed Kaminov, heard the phone ring in his office at 8:30 A.M.

"We have Harvey Weinstein," said a male voice. The caller set the ransom at $3 million: $2 million in $100 bills and the remainder in $50 bills. He told Kaminov that the kidnappers were part of an international ring known as the Black Cat Organization. "We'll be in touch with you," the kidnapper said and hung up.

Weinstein's four children—Mark, 36; Debby, 35; Lori, 39; and Dan, 31—scrambled to pull together the ransom while other calls from his abductors came in. The callers promised that they would release Weinstein three hours after they had the money in their hands. But it turned out not be be that simple.

On the second day of Weinstein's captivity, a micro-cassette recorder was dropped down, and he was ordered to send a message to his children. He tried to give some clues to where he was in the tape.

After griping about not having cigarettes, Weinstein said, "You can't see me from topside." It was a clue that he was underground, although detectives didn't know whether it meant he was in ship or in a hole.

On August 7, three days after the kidnapping, Mark, following the caller's directions, tried to deliver the ransom. He drove to a spot on New York City's Grand Central Parkway, the place designated by the kidnappers, and looked for a signal, a car with flashing lights. But none came.

Later there was another call, and another rendezvous was attempted. This time Mark carried the cash to a meeting place on the Henry Hudson Parkway. Again, he saw nothing, not a sign from the desperados who were holding "Mr. Harvey," as the callers referred to Weinstein.

That was the first clue to the identity of the kidnappers. "Mr. Harvey" was what Weinstein's workers called him, and it suggested that at least one of the kidnappers might be or had been an employee of the tuxedo king. But the police dared not follow up on this lead by checking the factory's 400-plus employees. They feared that it could put his life in jeopardy if his captors felt that they themselves were in danger or that the police were involved.

Negotiations were being conducted by Weinstein's daughter Lori and his cousin Ed Weinstein, a business executive. As far as the kidnappers knew, the police had not been called. In reality, more than 100 detectives were trying to find the victim, and had been since day one.

At least 50 calls from the kidnappers came in to Lori and Ed, who grew more concerned with each ring of the phone. On the other end, the key negotiator for the abductors, a woman, could barely speak English. Sometimes in frustration, she would start speaking in a foreign language, a dialect that stumped even linguistics experts at the United Nations.

Every day the kidnappers checked up on Weinstein. Light would filter in when his captors opened the cover slightly; they would toss food down a chute—bananas, plums, apples, and 12-ounce bottles of water—then disappear again. Sometimes they gave in to his pleas for a drag on their cigarettes. Other times they screamed at him and threatened to mutilate him or cut his body into pieces if his family didn't come up with the money.

Through it all, Weinstein kept a tight hold on the only thing he could control—himself. He carefully rationed his food. Food that was likely to rot quickly, like bananas and plums, was eaten right away, but, even though he was hungry, he held back on the water and other fruits. He knew that if he ate a lot, he would end up sitting in his own waste. Uneaten fruit and water were stored on his makeshift shelf, which was the ledge he had found at eye level.

Days were passing. He could tell that from the changes in the sound of the traffic from the nearby highway. By counting the number of times the roar of passing vehicles became heavy, he could calculate rush hours. It gave him an idea of how long he had been buried alive in the tomb.

Weinstein tried to exercise, using the walls for pushups and isometrics. But he believed that the key to survival was not physical. Weinstein was a tennis player, and he kept himself fit. He knew that it would take a lot before his body would fail. The real challenge was holding on to his mind, and to do that he had to keep busy.

Even though no one was around to hear him, he started shouting messages to his family and friends and even people like Janet Reno, then United States attorney general. "Janet, you need to get more agents out there!" he bellowed. "This is Harvey."

Mostly he talked to himself. *Don't panic, and you live*, he told himself over and over. It was something he had learned five decades earlier as an 18-year-old Marine during World War II. He had earned a Purple Heart and a Presidential Unit citation, among other medals, during brutal combat in the Pacific. If he could live through that hell, Weinstein told himself, he could live through this.

He started telling himself a story, the most interesting one he knew—his own. "This is the autobiography of Harvey Weinstein, beginning at age six," he announced. He told the story aloud, a little bit at a time, and marked off the chapters by drawing lines on the walls of his prison, even though it was too dark for him to see them.

Memories flooded back—how many there were astounded Weinstein, because he used to joke that he couldn't even remember what he ate for breakfast, even though he ate the same thing every day. Teachers and school chums from as early as first grade stood before him. High school sped by, as did his Marine Corps training and combat, even the time a shell exploded very near him. In other chapters he delved into raising his children and starting his business. Anything, any thought or memory, was pulled out of his memory bank to keep his mind off what was happening to him, or worse, what might happen next.

When he slept he dreamed of his new girlfriend, his children, even of playing tennis with his friend

David Dinkins, then mayor of New York City. He recalled passages from one of the last books he had read, Arthur Koestler's *Darkness at Noon,* whose subject, ironically, was prisoners in solitary confinement. Weinstein also depended heavily on his memories of Henry David Thoreau's masterpiece, *Walden,* especially the line "If I were confined in a garret, I would still possess the world."

Even so, despair crept into his mind from time to time. At one low point, he figured he would never get out alive. *They're better off leaving me in this crypt,* he thought. *They have no reason to free me— that would mean they're risking their lives.* When his captors returned he even pleaded with them to kill him and dump his body along a road, somewhere so his family could at least find him and know what had happened.

"Shoot me," he begged his abductors. But as usual, they just dropped some more fruit and water into his pit and went away.

After the first week, they gave him a plastic sheet and extra clothes as protection against the musty dampness and the rain that seeped in under the cover and turned the floor of the tomb into an excrement-filled, muddy quagmire. Weinstein had nowhere to defecate except where he slept and sat. But he managed to maintain a sliver of dignity by placing his food on the ledge.

The Chamber of Dread

While Weinstein struggled to stay calm in the underground cell, his family was growing frantic as attempts to deliver the ransom failed, one after another, for the most bizarre reasons. Once, Mark drove to the designated spot and blinked his headlights as he had been instructed to do. Two men approached the car but they were not the kidnappers. Instead, they were two gay men who mistook Mark's signal for an invitation.

Another time, Mark was driving to yet another ransom drop when he found himself in the midst of a high-speed police chase that had nothing to do with the kidnapping. All around him were squad cars with lights flashing, sirens blaring, and cops with guns drawn. It could have been a disaster if the kidnappers had believed that all the hubbub was for them. They might have thought that the police were closing in on them, and this could have been enough to convince them to drop negotiations and flee—or, worse yet, kill Weinstein.

The newspapers gave the police chase lots of coverage, but at the request of the police the press didn't print a word about Weinstein's kidnapping or the delicate negotiations throughout the crisis.

After one failed effort, Ed Weinstein, who had taken over handling the negotiations, came down hard on the abductors, berating them for botching the drops, cursing at them, and challenging them to prove that his cousin was still alive. The kidnappers slammed down the phone, and then there was not another word from them for 50 desperate hours.

The next call, on the morning of Saturday, August 14, was a bittersweet surprise. "This is Harvey," Weinstein told his cousin. "Sorry I'm putting you through what I'm putting you through. I'm in a hole." He was talking on a cell phone that had been lowered into his pit. Despite heavy static, so that he could hardly be heard, the message came through. Harvey Weinstein was not dead yet.

Another drop was arranged for Monday, August 16. Mark was given instructions to drive to Washington Heights and to look for a car flashing lights. The money was to be stashed in two black duffel bags. The kidnappers would release Weinstein three hours after they got their money.

For nine hours Mark, wired and wearing a bulletproof vest, cruised the neighborhood, tailed by rotating squads of plainclothes cops in beat-up old cars. Dawn came and nothing happened. It looked like another attempt to save his father had failed. Then at a stop sign near a park in upper Manhattan a man stepped out of the shadows. "Are you Mr. Mark?" he asked. Before Mark could answer, the man snatched the money and ran off into the park. Plainclothes police tailed him.

The Chamber of Dread

When the deadline to release Weinstein came and went, cops started making arrests. First nabbed was Fermin Rodriguez, 37, the man who picked up the bags. As detectives had suspected, Rodriguez worked for Weinstein. During the nearly two weeks since his boss had been kidnapped, Rodriguez had showed up every day at his post stitching tuxedos.

Nobody at Lord West suspected anything. But Rodriguez's wife knew something was wrong. She had noticed that her husband had changed over the past several months from a hard-working family man to someone she didn't know, someone mean and unpredictable. Rodriguez had started beating her, so she had learned to stop asking him questions. When she noticed him coming home late at night covered in mud, she held her tongue for fear of being hit. She figured he was up to no good but she didn't know what.

Quickly the cops moved in. After picking up Rodriguez, they grabbed his brother Antonio, 28. Later they picked up a third suspect, a tough-looking 44-year-old woman, Aurelina Leonor. She was the woman who had made many of the phone calls. She was also Rodriguez's girlfriend.

Police learned that the trio had plane tickets to the Dominican Republic. They had planned to take the ransom money and run, leaving their victim to die alone in his muddy crypt.

The cops suggested to Rodriguez that he had a choice. He could reveal the hiding spot and be charged with kidnapping, or he could keep his mouth shut and let Weinstein die. This would bring him a murder rap. Rodriguez wisely chose to tell them where to find the victim.

A few hours after the arrests, Detectives William Mondore and Ruben Santiago were scouring the woody, garbage-strewn area near a park in upper Manhattan, yelling, "Mr. Weinstein! Mr. Weinstein!" At a point just yards from the Henry Hudson Parkway, they heard a faint reply.

"I'm over here!" Weinstein shouted from his pit. They followed the voice to a pile of leaves covering wooden planks resting on cinder blocks. Mondore and Santiago pushed it all away and found a steel plate underneath. They lifted the plate and heard Weinstein's voice, stronger now, coming from out of the darkness below.

"Who are you?" Weinstein asked somewhat apprehensively.

"Police," Mondore replied. "Are you Harvey Weinstein?"

"Yes, yes I am! Just let me hold your hand."

Mondore saw four fingers emerging into the light. The detective grabbed the hand and pulled the weary, filthy businessman out of the pit that had been his tomb for 13 agonizing days. Weinstein was caked with mud and had dropped 18 pounds from his trim frame. But he was alive.

"Oh, my God, thank you," Weinstein gushed. In almost the same breath he asked, "Do you smoke?" Then he bummed a cigarette. "God, I love the New York City Police Department. And I'm sure glad to see the daylight."

After receiving a medical checkup and being reunited with his relieved family, Weinstein faced a new concern. Almost immediately he was being buried again, this time with offers for movies, books, and articles about the ordeal. Weinstein turned them all down. Before the kidnapping he had been a successful, low-profile businessman, well known among tuxedo manufacturers, but not in other circles. He wanted to take his place again out of the spotlight.

All the ransom money was recovered. The three kidnappers later were convicted and received life sentences.

Within a few days of being given his freedom, the man for whom the whole city of New York was praying returned to his old routine for the first time since his abduction. He drove to the Mark Twain Diner, where Corrine the waitress again served his raisin bran, followed up by her "stop smoking" lecture. Then it was on to his factory, where his employees greeted their boss with hugs, tears, and cheers.

"Harvey! Harvey!" they chanted happily, as a beaming Weinstein passed through the doors, back to the life he had almost lost. He told his workers, "While I was in that hole, the Lord, through your prayers, watched over me. Without that, I wouldn't have made it."

THE LIGHTHOUSE NIGHTMARE

Everything seemed to be smooth sailing to the mariners who guided their ships past the lighthouse at Stratford Shoals in the middle of Long Island Sound in August 1905. The white beam from the great oil lantern never went dark as it helped guide the ships through the treacherous rocks and sandbars.

No seaman who peered through the dark toward the lonely light could have guessed that inside the lighthouse a man was fighting for his life, desperately trying to fend off a murderous maniac for nearly a week.

When that week began there was no hint that Assistant Lighthouse Keeper Morrell Hulse, 55, was about to face six days of hell—six days in which his very survival depended upon keeping his wits and staying awake.

Hulse's boss, Head Keeper Gilbert Ruland, had scheduled a vacation for the week of July 31, and he had arranged for a substitute, an experienced lighthouse man named Julius Coster, to take his spot and team up with Hulse. Hulse had worked with the portly, cheerful, middle-aged Coster before and was happy to see him arrive in the boat that shuttled the keepers from the shore to the lighthouse, which was located in the narrow passage between Port Jefferson, Long Island, and Bridgeport, Connecticut. The octagonal 35-foot granite tower stood on a 30-foot granite base and was attached to a two-story keeper's house.

When they greeted each other, Hulse noticed that his partner appeared to be his usual friendly self, just a bit tired and distracted, not much interested in chatting. During the first few hours, Coster settled into his quarters and went to bed. He was supposed to get up at dawn Tuesday to give Hulse a much-needed break from the all-consuming task of tending the light.

Hulse was nearing the end of his shift early Tuesday, when suddenly he heard loud shrieks coming from the first floor of the attached keeper's house. Hulse rushed down to Coster's room, but at the threshold he was met with an alarming sight. There at the door stood Coster, pale and sweating. His wide eyes were burning with madness.

The Lighthouse Nightmare

In his hand Coster held a boat hook to which he had lashed a straightedge razor. When Coster's bulging, bloodshot eyes caught sight of Hulse, he charged him, wildly flailing with the razor-equipped boat hook. Hulse ducked as the weapon whipped past him perilously close to his head.

Although Coster continued his maniacal assault, it was no longer aimed at his fellow keeper. Instead, the madman charged about the lighthouse, screaming and slashing at enemies only he could see. "Spirits, be damned! Leave! I command you!" He kept up his crazy attack from morning until dusk, sometimes threatening Hulse by waving his makeshift weapon at him; other times flailing madly at the air.

Around nightfall on Tuesday, Coster, his strength sapped, slumped into a sweating, gasping heap, his eyes still wide and wild. Soon he drifted off into a fitful sleep.

Trembling with fear and exhausted from trying to ward off his attacker for nearly 12 hours, Hulse considered his situation. This being the age before telephones were installed in lighthouses, there was no way for him to reach anyone on the shore, no way to signal for help.

If he stayed at the lighthouse, Hulse would have to overpower and then somehow restrain his hefty coworker. Failing that, Hulse knew he'd have to remain awake and maintain a constant state of high alert, tensely awaiting Coster's next violent outburst until help arrived. That would be in no less than six days, when the head keeper was scheduled to return. No one else was slated to come to the lighthouse before then. Hulse had serious doubts that he could fight off sleep—and Coster—for that long.

The safest and sanest course of action would be to flee the lighthouse and try to swim to shore, leaving Coster alone to battle it out with his imaginary demons. Hulse considered this possibility for a moment, but he discarded it. He was not the kind of man who could desert his post and risk hundreds of lives aboard the big steamers that every night crossed the dangerous waters of Long Island Sound. *No,* Hulse thought, *I couldn't live with myself knowing I'd put other lives in danger. I've got to stay on and keep the lamp lit. Perhaps Coster is suffering some kind of nervous breakdown and he'll get over it soon and the steady fellow I know will return to his old self again.*

Comforting though this thought was, it was erased from Hulse's mind Wednesday evening by the sound of frenzied banging in the keeper's quarters on the lower level. Hulse inched down the narrow spiral staircase to witness a bizarre scene.

There was Coster with a hammer, chisel, and his razor-backed boat hook trying to hack a hole in the lighthouse wall. "Demon! Demon!" he bellowed when

The Lighthouse Nightmare

he saw Hulse staring at him from the stairs. To Hulse's relief, Coster turned his attention away from the lighthouse keeper and continued hacking at the wall instead.

"The light! We have to put out the light! It's drawing the demons!" Coster screamed as he chopped away.

Hulse made no effort to interfere with his partner's violent redecorating project. *I'd better leave him alone,* Hulse thought. *As long as he's busy hacking away at the wall then he won't be trying another attack against me. Besides, it's getting dark and I'd better man the light and worry about Coster later.*

Coster ranted and raved Wednesday night and into Thursday morning before he fell asleep. Hulse tried to get some rest, too, but found it almost impossible because of his fear that he could be attacked at any moment.

Hulse was trapped in the lighthouse, sharing a cramped space with a lunatic who inexplicably had murder on his mind. Hulse knew it would take all of his own strength and will to survive. The sun was going down as he started his fourth day without sleep—four days of tensely waiting for the maniac to strike.

When Coster awoke Thursday evening he began pounding on the wall again while the fatigued Hulse kept watch over the light. Sometime during the night, the banging stopped, and Hulse felt a double-edged comfort from the silence. He was relieved by the quietness but he was also concerned about what Coster might do next.

Hulse was so exhausted that his eyelids grew heavy. He blinked, then blinked again and again. Each time his eyes stayed closed just a little bit longer. In the lull, Hulse did what he swore he wouldn't do—he fell asleep.

He was jolted back to consciousness by a different kind of pounding. Once he fully woke up, Hulse realized that the light had stopped revolving. Then he spotted Coster again, this time with an ax, driving spikes into the machinery that rotated the light. As soon as Coster noticed Hulse, the madman raised the ax over his head as he prepared to strike a blow that would shatter the great lens.

Although dog-tired from lack of sleep, Hulse leaped at the ax-wielding lunatic, wrestled him to the ground, and knocked him out. For the rest of the night, Hulse kept vigil over the revolving beacon and the slumbering attacker.

When Coster awoke Friday morning, he was still in a frenzy, but this time his violence was directed at a new demon. Grabbing the razor, he started hacking at himself with the same intensity he had directed against Hulse, the imaginary demons, and the bricks of the lighthouse. But by this time the razor was about as sharp as a sea-smoothed pebble, and despite his frantic jabs and slashes, Coster managed to raise just a few welts and surface cuts on himself.

Then he attempted to end his own life by grabbing a kitchen knife and stabbing himself. Hulse tried to stop him but Coster shoved him aside. Although he succeeded in giving himself a few deep cuts, Coster was too weak to commit suicide. He even tried to whack himself with the ax, but his strength had left him. Soon he and Hulse became so exhausted that all the two men could do was slump to the floor and stare at one another.

For the next three nights, Hulse, near delirious with exhaustion, unwaveringly staggered to his post and kept watch over the light, all the while staying alert for any movement of the madman. During the days, Hulse made sure to keep all weapons away from Coster, although he let him continue to attack the wall with a blunt boat hook.

Hulse made it through Sunday night and into dawn on Monday. But by now, he had reached a stage beyond fatigue. He collapsed. Then, as if in a dream, he heard a new sound accompanying the morning light. It wasn't Coster's incessant pounding. No, this was the voice of Head Light Keeper Gilbert Ruland alerting the lighthouse tenders of his return.

Hulse gathered up all the strength he could summon and met Ruland at the dock and explained his hellish week-long ordeal. Together the two men easily overpowered Coster and strapped him down. Then Ruland rowed him back to shore.

No one could say what had driven Coster mad, but word was that he had gone on a week-long bender in Port Jefferson, something not uncommon for men who might be cooped up in a lighthouse for weeks on end. He was immediately dismissed from service and put on a train out of town, and no one heard from him again.

After sleeping for 24 hours straight, Hulse was soon back at his post manning the lighthouse.

THE HIDDEN VALLEY HORROR

It started out as a once-in-a-lifetime sightseeing flight. It ended in a life-and-death struggle for survival.

On May 13, 1945, several members of the Far East Air Service Command in Dutch New Guinea were invited to enjoy a Sunday afternoon excursion over Hidden Valley, a real-life Shangri-la deep in the interior and cut off from the outside world by soaring, picturesque jungle-covered mountains. Pilots who had flown over the area had told their colleagues at the base tales of seeing extraordinary sights: savage warriors, seven-foot-tall cannibals, and exotic native Dorothy Lamour look-alikes.

Eager to get the finest view on the flight, Corporal Maggie Hastings, a diminutive 30-year-old Wac (Women's Army Corps member), was the first to board the twin-prop C-47 (a DC-3 hybrid). The seat behind the pilot seemed to be the best bet, but when she looked out the window she was disappointed by the poor view. So she hurriedly checked out the other seats before settling on one in the last row just as the other passengers began to board.

Two other Wacs, Private Eleanor Hanna and Sergeant Laura Besley, sat down in the rear near Maggie. So did Sergeant Kenneth Decker, a lanky 36-year-old from Kelso, Washington, who had asked Maggie out on a date just weeks earlier but had been turned down. The last to board were the McCollom twins, Robert and John, both 26-year-old lieutenants from Trenton, Missouri. Robert took the remaining seat in the front of the cabin, and John took the seat next to Maggie.

With its capacity load of 24 passengers—eight women and 16 men—the plane lifted off and soon soared over the Oranje Mountains, a range of steep jungle-green slopes. In less than an hour, the plane reached the exotic Hidden Valley. As the aircraft swooped down to within three hundred feet of the valley floor, Maggie gazed at the beautiful sight below, not knowing what to expect after all the stories she had heard from pilots. But the valley was filled with carefully tended farm fields, and neat round huts with thatched roofs, not at all suited to seven-foot-tall savage cannibals.

After a couple of low sightseeing passes, the

plane started its climb out of the picturesque valley. But suddenly, at about 9,000 feet, it began to shake violently. Maggie looked out the window and gasped. The tail of the big plane was shearing the tops off the trees near the peak of a jungle-clad mountain.

"Give her the gun and let's get out of here!" her seatmate, John McCollom, shouted.

Seconds later, the passengers were rocked by an enormous bang as the transport slammed into the mountainside. Their shrieks of alarm and the crumpling of twisting metal were drowned out by two huge explosions, one after another. The plane bounced hard three times before it finally came to rest.

Flames were licking at Maggie's hair and burning her face as she fell to her knees and hurriedly crawled away from the white-hot blaze. She found an opening in the cracked fuselage and tumbled out onto the ground. After scurrying to a safe distance, she turned around and looked in horror at the burning tomb that seconds earlier had been a plane holding 24 thrilled passengers on a Sunday afternoon excursion.

Tears welled in her eyes the moment she realized how incredibly lucky she was. When the plane crashed, its tail snapped off, leaving a gaping hole for her to escape through. Her decision to sit in the back of the plane saved her life—and also that of

John McCollom, who rushed over to her. Amazingly, he didn't have a scratch on him.

Before they could say a word to each other, they heard a woman's desperate cry for help. McCollom dashed back into the flames and pulled a hysterically screaming Laura Besley to safety. Then he rushed again into the inferno and carried out her seatmate, Eleanor Hanna, who was unconscious and badly burned.

After gently laying her on the ground, he charged toward the burning craft again, hoping to go to the front section to save his twin brother, Robert. But by now the flames were too intense and blocked his way, forcing him to reluctantly turn back.

Meanwhile a fifth survivor, Sergeant Kenneth Decker, had emerged from the burning plane. As he staggered toward the small group, he grumbled, "Helluva way to spend your birthday." Decker had turned 36 that day. When he reached Maggie, she was startled to see that smoke was actually rising from Decker's back and blood was slithering down his face from a forehead gash so deep she could see his skull.

At first Maggie was unaware that she herself had been seriously hurt. She could see a deep laceration on her left hand, but for half an hour she failed to notice the deep cut in her foot and the burns on her face and legs. She was still in too much shock to feel any pain or realize that some of her hair had burned off and that she also had lost her shoes.

Because the fire was spreading, the survivors knew they were still too close to be out of danger. With McCollom cradling the limp Eleanor in his arms, they all hustled to the relative safety of a ledge about 25 yards away.

The dazed group sat shivering in stunned silence, except for Laura, who was still screaming. A chilly rain started to fall, soaking their clothes, but at least it extinguished the fires. McCollom soon went back into the plane and returned, soberly telling the survivors what they knew in their hearts—all the other passengers had died.

McCollom salvaged what he could from the plane's interior, hauling out a signal kit, some yellow tarpaulins, a few cans of water, vitamins, morphine, and hard candies. He put a tarp over Eleanor and Laura to shield them from the rain. Although there were no obvious signs of injury, Laura couldn't stop screaming. Eleanor just moaned, her breathing labored, her heart weakening. McCollom gave her some morphine to ease her agony and then joined Maggie and Decker under another tarp.

The next morning, he checked on the other two women. He returned and somberly announced, "Eleanor's dead." The others were too emotionally drained to cry. He carefully wrapped her body in a tarp and laid her by a tree. There was nothing else they could do.

After a few sips of water and pieces of hard candy, they decided to remain at the crash site for one more day before attempting to hike down to the valley because they needed more time to recover from their shock. They were still shaking uncontrollably, none more so than Laura. Even morphine didn't seem to help her. Although Decker didn't complain, it was obvious he was in great pain from his wounds.

Around midmorning they heard a search plane overhead, but the jungle canopy was too dense for the stranded party to be seen from the air. McCollom tried signaling with a mirror, but with no luck. What they didn't know until later was that they had crashed in an area so remote that it was labeled "unknown" on all Army maps.

Late that afternoon rain fell again, so Maggie and Laura huddled together under a tarp. Before dozing off, Maggie analyzed her chances of survival. She understood that if they were to live, they needed to move. But she worried about how she would negotiate the wild terrain barefoot.

An hour later, Maggie woke up and became frightened when she noticed that Laura wasn't breathing. She yelled for McCollom, who felt for Laura's pulse. There was none. Then without saying a word he wrapped her in another tarp and gently placed her by Eleanor's body.

Maggie mourned for her two friends, but a practical thought intruded on her grief: *Now Laura's shoes belong to me.*

The next morning, Maggie, Decker, and McCollom began their trek down the jungle mountain in hopes of reaching a village. It was a scary thought, of course, especially in light of the stories they'd heard about giant cannibals, but there was nothing else to do. They could either try to reach a village and perhaps die at the hands of savages or stay on the mountain, where they were sure to die. The trio chose the unknown.

The branches and leaves were so dense that it was hard to beat a path through them. Maggie found it particularly difficult because her long blond hair was constantly getting tangled in branches, stopping all progress as she twisted and pulled and yanked it free. Finally it became too much. She asked McCollom to hack it all off with his pocketknife. He chopped her locks until her hair was only about two inches long.

But there was another problem, one that was worsening by the moment, and for this McCollum had no easy fixes. The wounds and burns on his two companions were quickly becoming infected. It was just a matter of time before gangrene and maggots set in. As their pain increased, Maggie and Decker found it harder and harder to battle through the jungle.

Slowly they worked their way down through the jungle brush. At one point they swung Tarzan-like on vines to lower themselves from a 12-foot drop into a stream. Hour after hour they marched. The diminutive WAC, struggling to keep up with her taller companions, was beginning to fade. To keep her going, the men goaded and chided her. Decker cursed her and called her a quitter. She got so mad that she vowed that she'd get through this nightmare no matter what it took.

After hiking for five hours, they reached a clearing; here Maggie collapsed on the ground. As she lay there facedown, McCollom spread out the bright yellow tarpaulins, hoping to been seen by a search plane. It worked. Within an hour a plane flew overhead and the pilot tipped his wings to the cheering, waving survivors—including Maggie, who felt rejuvenated by the sound of those engines.

A prompt rescue, however, was not in the cards. The terrain was too rough for a plane to safely land. The best the trio could hope for was a supply drop with food, water, a radio, and medicine and bandages to treat the festering wounds on Maggie and Decker. So they sat there waiting for help to arrive, joking and laughing to pass the time and take their minds off of the horror of what they had left behind.

Soon they heard a weird noise like a pack of yapping dogs. But quickly they realized the sounds were coming from humans. The natives had found them. Maggie saw one head emerge from the foliage, then another and another, until at least 100 short, dark-skinned, muscular men, some smeared with a smelly black goo, were peering at the strangers. All of them, Maggie noticed, had enormous flat feet. Each man was clad in nothing but a thong with a gourd in front and a leaf covering the rear. Almost all carried stone axes. They wore long hairnets of heavy string that stretched down their backs and held many possessions.

Although the natives were far shorter than the alleged giant cannibals of the region, the three survivors were still frightened, although they put on a friendly appearance. McCollom, Maggie, and Decker smiled broadly and held out peace offerings: their meager supplies and Maggie's compact. The three kept smiling as the natives closed in on them; the men huddled together and talked fast in an odd, clipped language. Then the leader, older than the rest, walked slowly closer to the trio. When he was right in front of McCollom, he smiled and held out his hand. He was gesturing for a handshake. Now the smiles were for real.

The natives took the peace offerings, looked at them, and laughed at the sight of themselves in the compact mirror. But when they were through they returned the items. They built a fire and all shared a smoke before the natives left.

A supply plane roared overhead the next day and dropped packages of food, medicine, and a two-way radio. McCollom reported details of the crash and was told that medics would be dropped by parachute as soon as possible. Until then, the threesome would have to get by as best they could.

They tried to keep their spirits up by taking good-natured jibes at each other. Gazing at Maggie's singed eyebrows and her hair, which stood straight up in short tufts, Decker teased, "Maggie, you are certainly a Sad Sack."

Pointing to their dirty clothes and four-day beards, she taunted back, "Neither one of you is exactly a Van Johnson." (They were referring to, respectively, a comic strip character and a movie star.)

McCollom was in pain from a cracked rib—which he did not reveal to his fellow survivors—but he nevertheless tended to Decker and Maggie, whose infections were getting worse. Maggie knew that her feet and hand were showing signs of gangrene and she feared that she might lose her legs if help didn't come soon. But she kept her worries to herself. Decker was in even worse shape. Not until he took off his clothes and lay facedown did the other two realize what pain he must be suffering in silence. The bad burns over his back and legs had turned gangrenous. It was agony for him to have McCollom put ointment on the infected areas. But Decker didn't complain once.

By nightfall, McCollom was teetering on the brink of exhaustion, Maggie was too sick and weak to move, and Decker was dying. Time was running out.

The next day, a plane dropped more supplies, including new rations. The three all reached for the same thing—the canned bacon and eggs. But they were too sick to finish eating them.

Late in the day, the natives' leader, whom McCollom nicknamed Pete, returned with a group of women dressed only in G-strings made of twigs. They carried with them their local delicacies of sweet potatoes, green bananas, and a pig. These people, whom Maggie had feared as savage cannibals, wanted nothing more than to make a dinner party for their guests. But the survivors were too ill to partake, so Pete and his followers went home.

In the middle of the night, a tropical storm dumped heavy rains, forcing Maggie to join the two men who were on higher ground. "Lord," groaned McCollom, "are we never to get rid of this woman?"

At noon two medical paratroopers parachuted in two miles away in the valley where the terrain wasn't so dangerous. (The base had no helicopters.) They made their way to the survivors and immediately began treatment. For the next six hours, the medics carefully scraped encrusted gangrene off Maggie's and Decker's wounds. During an exam, the docs discovered that Decker had suffered a broken elbow. The medical remedies were painful, but Maggie was determined to be as stoic as Decker. Both refused to whimper or groan despite the agony they endured.

That night the medics built a fire and made the survivors hot chocolate and their first hot meal in nearly a week. On Sunday, a week after the crash, more supplies were dropped, including a rosary for Maggie, a prayer book for McCollom, and a Bible for Decker. Later in the day Maggie felt good enough to take her first bath in a week in a stream. She walked away from the camp behind a knoll and stripped. As she soaped herself up, she had the feeling that she wasn't alone. She looked around and there, on a neighboring knoll, were dozens of natives watching her every move.

A few days later six more paratroopers arrived to help the survivors. Then an Army plane dropped the most heartbreaking supplies of all: 20 crosses, one Star of David, and 21 dog tags for the burial of the victims of the crash. Several paratroopers went to the scene of the accident and put up the star and crosses. Meanwhile, back at the camp, the rest sat around the two-way radio and listened sadly as Catholic, Protestant, and Jewish chaplains read burial services for the dead.

Once the medical danger had passed for the survivors, the big question remained: How would they all get out of there? Rescuers couldn't drive in or land a plane, and the base had no helicopter. The survivors couldn't walk out. The only solution was to build an airstrip. Even so, there was no place flat and long enough for a regular plane to land and take off. But a glider could do it in a much smaller area. Unfortunately, the nearest clearing was in another part of the valley nearly 50 miles away.

The plan called for three paratroopers to drop into that clearing and build a runway. Then a glider would land there. They would attach to the nose of the glider a towline that looked like a giant loop suspended from two 10-foot poles about 50 yards away. After the survivors boarded the glider, a C-47, with a hook suspended from under its tail, would swoop down, snare the towline, and pull the glider out so it could fly the survivors back to civilization. It was an audacious, dangerous plan, but it was the only one that offered any real hope.

By mid-June, more than a month after the crash, the survivors and their escorts were ready to begin the long 50-mile hike to the now-completed airfield.

"Pete" and his tribe, who had been hanging

around the outsiders and enjoying their gifts, took the departure hard and followed down the path weeping as their new friends left. "They treated us like white gods dropped out of the sky," one paratrooper told Maggie.

The trek to the runway was arduous for Maggie and Decker, but neither complained, although it was obvious to the others how difficult it was for them. When they finally arrived at the new site, they rested up for a few days.

Finally, on June 28, more than six weeks after the crash, the day the survivors had been waiting for arrived. The glider drifted down to the makeshift airfield in Hidden Valley while a C-47 with the dubious nickname "Leaking Louise" circled overhead.

The passengers scrambled aboard the glider and held tight as the C-47 roared down in a power dive, hooked the glider's towrope, and started to climb. With a jolt, the glider headed down the runway and soon was airborne. But the drag on the C-47 was greater than expected and the big plane, its engines whining, strained to gain altitude. Its speed had decreased to only 105 miles an hour, slow enough to stall.

Meanwhile, with so little pulling power from the C-47, the glider grazed the treetops of the mountainside. Maggie clutched her rosary in fear and wondered, *I've survived a plane crash and suffered so much pain and hardship and sickness. And with my rescue so close am I going to die now?*

Fortunately, the C-47 found just enough power to maintain altitude and keep the glider in the air; ever so slowly it increased its speed and altitude until they had cleared the final mountain peak. Then both craft winged their way back to the base.

After they arrived, Decker was taken to the hospital. McCollom called his family to share the heartache of losing his twin brother. And Maggie made plans to go back to her hometown in Oswego, New York. But first, she had to do something she had been unable to do in Hidden Valley—weep for the loss of those who didn't survive.

THE CAST-OFF

Alone on a deserted island, Alexander Selkirk found himself battling an insidious enemy he had never known before. His very survival was at stake, yet he was losing the fight.

As a stalwart privateer he had without flinching bravely plundered Spanish galleons, weathered hurricanes, and brawled with fellow sailors twice his size. But what truly scared him now was the unrelenting, daunting foe that had been beating him down for months and months—total isolation.

It was unbearable, driving him mad, more so because he had only himself to blame. Selkirk was stuck alone on this far-flung isle not because he was a castaway but because he was a cast-off.

Selkirk, of Largo, Scotland, was an accomplished seaman who had taken part in several privateering expeditions—officially sanctioned piracy inflicted on

Britain's enemies, including the Spanish gold fleet and French shipping interests. In 1703 Selkirk, then 27, became sailing master (the person in charge of sailing the ship) aboard the *Cinque Ports,* an armed galley with 16 guns and 63 men. The ship joined forces with the 26-gun, 120-man *St. George* commanded by the famed navigator Captain William Dampier. After sailing out of Cork, Ireland, their mission was to hunt for Spanish ships off the coast of South America.

During the voyage the captain of the *Cinque Ports,* Charles Pickering, died and was replaced by the incompetent and abrasive Thomas Stradling. Almost immediately, Selkirk, hotheaded by nature, took an intense disliking to the new captain and began arguing with him over how to run the ship. Dampier sided with Selkirk, and he too quarreled with Stradling until the two captains ended their squabbling by steering their vessels in separate directions on May 19, 1704. Although he no longer had Dampier to back him up, Selkirk continued to clash with Stradling, especially over the seaworthiness of the ship.

Their quarrels, which continued for several more months, escalated as the *Cinque Ports* arrived at Juan Fernandez Island, about 400 miles due west of Valparaiso, Chile. Named after the Spanish sailor who discovered it in 1653, the island was a remote,

The Cast-off

uninhabited, 40 square miles of jagged, volcanic mountains covered by lush forests.

While the crew gathered wood and water for the ship, tempers mushroomed between Selkirk and the captain. Infuriated by Stradling's arrogance and ineptitude, Selkirk declared he would rather stay on the deserted island than remain on a leaky ship that he was sure would never make it back to England. In a huff, Selkirk hauled his belongings—including his chest, gun, and bedding—to the island. Then, using a deliberate pun, he told Stradling, "Rather than be straddled over by you any longer, I'm staying and taking my chances alone."

When the ship was ready to depart the island, Selkirk, who by now had had time to reflect on his rash decision, decided that sailing under a contemptuous captain was preferable to living alone on a secluded, wild island. So he swallowed his pride and asked Stradling to take him back.

Still fuming mad, Stradling refused. Filled with regret, on that September afternoon in 1704, Selkirk stood forlornly on the shore, watching the *Cinque Ports* grow smaller and smaller until it became a little speck on the horizon.

Selkirk was now alone. He had nothing but his meager belongings and his regrets. How much wiser it would have been, he thought, to put up with Stradling in silence than to be left in such a solitary dilemma. He had never heard a sound so dismal as the oars of the sailors who rowed away from the shore.

The first night, he slept under an overhanging rock. By the morning light, he made an inventory of what he had taken from the ship. It was not much. In addition to his bedding, chest of clothes, and nautical instruments, he had a hatchet, knife, kettle, gun, gun powder, tobacco, and some books, including a Bible.

After reading aloud from the Good Book, Selkirk caught and cooked a fish, then made a tour of the island. It was beautiful with abundant flowers and brightly colored birds that flew among high hills and crags. Bounding on the rocks were wild goats, descended from the first stock left by the island's namesake years earlier. Selkirk also found vegetables, the progeny of seeds from earlier visitors. The shallow waters provided plenty of shellfish too.

Even if he had to stay on the island forever, at least he would not starve. But now he needed to think less about the life he had forsaken and concentrate on the one he had so thoughtlessly chosen.

Selkirk, terrified by the prospect of looming isolation and loneliness, stayed in a cave near the beach during the first few weeks so he could keep his eyes glued to the horizon. He dared not abandon his position for fear of missing a passing ship. But when the beaches became invaded by hundreds of aggressive sea lions, he was forced to move inland for food and protection.

His new priority was shelter. He picked out a spot on high ground well back of the beach in a grove of shade trees. With his hatchet, he started the long, painstaking task of cutting down pimento trees and sharpening one end of each log so he could stick it into the earth and create a frame for his hut. At the top of each log he left a fork of two branches to serve as supports for sticks that he would lay horizontally to support his roof. A thick layer of long grass completed the roof. Then he shot and killed several goats and used their skins for the walls.

For his sleeping quarters, he carefully stacked sticks on the ground and covered them with grass and goat skins. Then he placed his bedding on top of it so he was far enough off the ground. Next, he built a separate hut for a kitchen and fashioned cups and bowls out of coconuts.

Working hard gave him a good appetite during the day and left him sleeping soundly at night. He made a rule never to sleep or work without first reading from the Bible. The comforting words made him feel he wasn't totally alone.

Even though he had food and shelter, Selkirk still couldn't rest easy. The island was teeming with huge rats that nipped at his toes and ears as he slept. They were descendants of rats that had come ashore long ago from buccaneers' ships. Fortunately, the same vessels had left other creatures—cats. A huge population of feral felines roamed the island.

Selkirk made the cats his allies by inviting them to dine, offering them fish and goat meat. Soon they were eating out of his hand and were ready to pounce on any beady-eyed rodent that threatened their two-legged friend.

Wanting to have fresh milk, Selkirk devised a way to tame several goats. He deliberately shot at the leg of a kid to make it lame. Then he captured the animal and brought it to his shelter where he tied it up. Naturally, the mother followed. He fed the kid and the mother until they viewed him as their master. He repeated this method several more times until he had a large flock of tame goats that gave him not only fresh milk but companionship as well.

The cats made him less lonely too. He always made sure to share the milk with his cats, which over time multiplied into the hundreds. The felines and goats became so devoted to Selkirk that they followed him around the island and even slept by his bed.

The toughest part of surviving was trying to cope with the isolation. It gnawed at him constantly and often pitched him into a dark emotional hole that lasted for days. He was so desperate for human company that he talked to the cats and goats and sometimes even sang and danced for them. It took over a year before Selkirk was able to come to terms with his solitary situation.

Whenever he felt down, he counted his blessings. He had plenty of food, fresh water from a stream, decent shelter, and animal companions. He could make fire by rubbing sticks of pimento wood together. The weather was fine and there were only two months of winter, which brought mostly howling winds and cold rains. Other than suffering an occasional bout of dysentery or fever, Selkirk was in good health and in the best physical shape of his life. To keep busy, he fished, read, gathered food, and mended or made clothes.

He found the island to be laden with tasty fruits and vegetables, fish and fowl and goat meat. He learned to flavor his food with pepper berries and used cabbage palm as a substitute for bread.

Selkirk used one of the few nails he had saved from the ship as a needle to repair his clothes. He made a shirt out of a piece of linen he had in his chest. When his old clothes became too tattered to wear, he made a jacket and pants out of goat skin. When his knife wore out, he fashioned new ones out of the iron hoops of an old barrel that had washed ashore. He sharpened the blades by grinding them against a rock.

Eventually his shoes fell apart. But he didn't need them. The bottoms of his feet had become so hardened that he could run over rock and hard surfaces just as easily as the goats did.

One of his favorite pastimes was chasing wild goats. Having run out of gunpowder, he needed a new way to catch them—so he raced after them. He became a surprisingly speedy, nimble runner who eventually was faster than the goats. When he would catch one for the fun of it, he cut a slit in its ear to mark it and then let it go. Over time, he counted nearly one thousand whose ears had felt his knife.

One day Selkirk caught a goat that had fled to the brink of a cliff concealed by bushes. As he seized the goat, they both fell off the edge. The impact upon landing knocked Selkirk out cold. When he regained consciousness the next day, he found that he had been saved from possible death or serious injury because he had landed on the goat, which had died in the fall.

Bruised and battered, the pain-wracked Selkirk stumbled slowly back to his shelter, where he lay for ten days without anybody or anything to help relieve his suffering. Never before had he felt the need for another human, someone who could nurse him and comfort him. Eventually he recovered from his injuries, although his heart craved companionship.

Selkirk kept track of the passage of time by carving notches in a tree to mark the days, weeks, and months. He regularly climbed a volcanic peak and searched the vast expanse of blue sea for any signs of a passing ship, hoping and praying that this would be the day when he hailed a vessel that would take him off the island. He even had ready a stack of kindling at his lookout to build a signal fire.

A year went by, then two, without a single sign of another human being. Then one day, his greatest hope seemed realized. A ship was heading toward the island!

Thrilled by the sight, he started to prepare the fire. But his excitement quickly turned to dread when he realized that it was a Spanish ship—an enemy ship. He didn't dare light a fire. He would rather remain alone on the island than be captured and turned into a slave toiling in a South American mine. The vessel sailed on without incident.

A few months later, while he was napping near the shore, a Spanish ship actually landed. This time he was spotted by the sailors, who were shocked to see a strange, hairy two-legged beast in goat skins. They gave chase with their dogs and began shooting at him as he frantically fled into the forest. He climbed to the top of a large tree and hid among the thick leaves and branches as he watched the Spaniards stop directly under him. They stayed at that spot long enough to kill and dress a goat, but they didn't realize he was perched above them the whole time. He felt immense relief when they returned to their ship and sailed away.

Quiet solitude returned to the island and remained that way as the third year passed, and the fourth.

Then one day, while casting his gaze over the ocean as he had so many other times in vain, he gasped in astonishment. Two ships were sailing past the island. Trying hard to keep his exhilaration in check in case they were Spanish vessels, he waited for several excruciating minutes until he could identify them. To his boundless rapture, they were English.

Trembling with happy anticipation, he hurriedly started a large fire to signal them. The crews saw the smoke, and soon the British privateers *Duke*, commanded by Captain Woodes Rogers, and *Duchess*, commanded by Captain William Courtney, arrived on the island. It was February 2, 1709—more than four years and four months since Selkirk had seen a friendly human face.

At first Captain Rogers didn't know what to think of the lost soul of Juan Fernandez Island. Who was this dark-skinned, shaggy-haired savage in goat skins? Selkirk didn't help matters any when he discovered that since he hadn't conversed over the last four years, he now had trouble speaking and telling his tale.

But then he burst into a happy cry when he recognized one of the sailors: his friend Captain Dampier, the shipmaster who back in 1704 had been so fed up with Captain Stradling that he went his own way. Dampier vouched for Selkirk, declaring the wild-looking man was the best sailing master he knew.

That night Selkirk prepared a big dinner for his guests, serving them roasted goat, boiled cabbage, goat's milk, fruit, and fish. Never had he felt so jubilant, so ecstatic. The lone cast-off was among friends, fellow sailors, who would free him from his lengthy solitary existence.

When the day came to leave the island—the day he had dreamed about for nearly four and a half years— Selkirk felt surprisingly melancholy because he was leaving behind everything that had become dear to him since he had been a cast-off. He bade a sad farewell to the crude hut and kitchen he had built, the tools and utensils he had fashioned, and the clothes he had sewn. He said goodbye to the stream that had provided him with fresh water, the meadow where he had taken his afternoon naps, the lookout site that led to his deliverance. But what tugged at his heart the most was saying goodbye to his family of goats and cats—loyal companions who had given him such immense pleasure and asked so little in return.

As his ship began to head for the open sea, Selkirk turned around to cast one last glance toward the place where he had learned how to commune with nature and converse with God; how to survive with a strong heart and a clever mind. If his incredible experience did nothing more, it at least made him a better man than when he arrived there.

For a while, Selkirk had trouble adjusting to life aboard ship. He had lost his taste for coffee, tea, and alcohol and gagged on these beverages, much to the amusement of the crew. He hated the unhealthy food that was served. Shoes made his feet swell.

He had so much to learn, so much catching up to do. One of the first things he asked about was the fate of the ship that had stranded him. The *Cinque Ports,* he was told, had sunk after springing leaks shortly after Selkirk was set ashore. Almost all the crew drowned, and those who didn't—including the despised Captain Stradling—had been taken prisoner by the Spaniards and left to rot in a jail in Peru.

Rogers appointed Selkirk master's mate of the *Duke.* For the next two years, he and his shipmates engaged in a series of privateering raids along the coasts of Peru and Chile, amassing a small fortune.

Not until late 1711—eight years after he had originally embarked on the *Cinque Ports*—did Selkirk return to Scotland, shocking his relatives who had long given him up for dead. He tried to settle down, and even got married, but the lure of the sea proved too strong for him and he was off again. He died in 1721 of yellow fever aboard ship off the coast of Africa.

The Cast-off

But that's not the end of his story. After Selkirk's return home Captain Rogers wrote about the sailor's odyssey. The story caught the eye of a writer of mostly political books, pamphlets, and poems, like "Ode to the Pillory," a satire written while he was in prison for taking the wrong side against the government. By the time he read Rogers's account, the author was sick and nearly broke, and decided to try something new. So he wrote a novel that was inspired by Selkirk's adventures.

The writer was Daniel Defoe, and his book, published in 1719, became a classic tale of survival—*The Adventures of Robinson Crusoe.*

TRIAL
BY
BALLOON

Conditions were good for the flight of Navy Balloon A-5598 when it floatcd off in the late afternoon of Monday, December 13, 1920, from the U.S. Naval Air Station at Rockaway Beach, New York. Skies were clear and winds were mild. There was no sign of the vicious storm that would soon blow the three pilots into an icy death grip.

Carrying Lieutenants A. J. Kloor, Walter Hinton, and Stephen Farrell in a rattan basket, the rising 35,000-cubic-foot hydrogen balloon headed north in a test flight. The men had rations for a day: a couple of bottles of coffee, eight sandwiches, chocolate bars, and packages of crackers. It was more than enough for the trip. Or so it seemed.

The men expected an ordinary little balloon hop. For directions, they brought along a railway map provided by the Quebec Central Railroad. They planned to figure out their location by following the tracks. The plan was to hook onto an air stream that would carry them north over the Adirondack Mountains of upstate New York. They were wearing their flying suits; they hadn't bothered to put on electrically heated protective clothing.

When they took off, they had 21 30-pound bags of sand to use as ballast. They also were carrying a cage of four carrier pigeons to use for sending messages back to the naval station.

As they climbed above New York City, they marveled at the sight of the Brooklyn Bridge and released one of the pigeons over the Brooklyn Navy Yard. Soon, however, there were no more sights to see because thick, gray clouds had formed a floor under them, blocking their view of the world below. With no visibility, they had to determine their position solely by compass.

Although not the ideal way to navigate, it wasn't particularly worrisome to the three aeronauts. All were Navy aces with countless dangerous journeys by balloon or airplane under their belts. In fact, Hinton, who was flying in a balloon for the first time, had been a member of the crew of the NC-4 Flying Boat which had made the world's first transatlantic flight in 1919.

About eight P.M., after about three hours of traveling through the fog and darkness, the three balloonists descended to get their bearings and found

Trial by Balloon

themselves near a little town. They moored their huge floating craft to the top of a tree and startled a man who was walking below them.

"Hello!" Kloor called out. "Where are we?"

"Wells, New York," the surprised stroller yelled back, peering up into the cloudy night sky at the massive whitish shape above him.

The fliers had never heard of the town. "Where's the nearest city?" Kloor asked.

"Don't know, I can't really say for sure," the man replied.

For a moment they considered setting down in Wells, but decided against it. Kloor, the youngest and greenest of the group, was in command on this trip and was eager to complete his mission. He wasn't about to let a little fog get in his way. So they untied their balloon and lifted off again.

Spirits were light as they skimmed at around 30 miles per hour over the earth through the clouds in the silent craft. Christmas was on their minds. Both Hinton and Farrell were married men with children and were looking forward to spending the holidays at home with their families.

Kloor, dubbed "The Kid" by his fellow crew members, was 22 and the only bachelor member of the trio, although he had recently decided to embark on a journey perhaps more perilous than anything he could encounter in the air. Just weeks earlier he had become engaged to the lovely Alexandra Flowerton, who lived on Manhattan's Upper East Side.

The balloonists had begun munching on their food and were trading jibes in the dark, when suddenly an unexpected gust slammed into the balloon, practically pushing it on its side and changing the frail craft's course. The gust turned into a steady, hard wind that blew in a driving rain. Icy droplets tasting of salt stung the aeronauts' eyes and caked their clothes. The cold rain fell for hours as the wind shoved the balloon at more than 60 miles an hour.

Around midnight, the craft dipped briefly under the clouds just long enough for the men to see the lights of what looked like a large town. Again they debated setting down but again decided against it, figuring the worst was over and the rains would end in a few hours. They ate more sandwiches and drank more coffee as they brought the balloon higher and continued to lurch through the storm.

By daybreak the rains had let up and the clouds cleared enough for the men to get a bird's-eye view of the landscape below them. They looked out over an expanse of forests, lakes, and snow but saw no sign of human life. The balloonists had no idea where they were.

The temperature started to drop, and the balloon, kept aloft by hydrogen, started to descend quickly as the hydrogen's volume contracted.

Trial by Balloon

"Get light! Get light!" Kloor shouted as their rattan basket scraped noisily against the tops of the trees. "Dump the sand!"

Frantically, the three men hoisted bag after bag of the ballast overboard, until the craft started to gain a little altitude. But it wasn't enough, so the men quickly looked around the tiny basket for more things to toss out. First to go was the heavy, long drag rope, essential to let the balloonists know when they were getting too close to the tree tops. Because the rope was the heaviest thing on board, they cut it up and dumped it out. Next went thermos bottles, seats, carpets, even the lining of the basket. The compass, altimeter and other instruments were about to go over when Farrell thought better of it and decided to hold on to them for just a bit longer. The delicate instruments might come in handy.

"We're in bad," Farrell murmured. The other two men glanced at him but said nothing. Then their predicament took a turn for the worse. At that moment, the sun burst out from behind the clouds, and now the hydrogen gas in the balloon started to warm and expand. With nothing to hold it down, the balloon quickly soared to 6,500 feet, and drifted in a northwesterly direction.

As far as the men could see there was still no sign of human life until half past noon when they spotted what they thought was a little shack, and perhaps salvation. But they couldn't be sure, flying at that height and at that speed. It might just as well have been a big boulder.

Then a faint sound reached the craft. "Do you hear that?" Hinton whispered. They listened again.

"It's a dog," Kloor declared. The others nodded. Even at such a great height, they were sure they had heard a barking dog. "Where there's a dog, there's often a man and a chance for survival. We're going to set down."

The only way to do it was to release hydrogen and risk a crash landing. Over the next half hour Kloor released hydrogen three times and the balloon descended. It slammed into the tops of trees, dragging the rattan basket for 20 feet and smashing it to bits. Fortunately, none of the men was thrown out or hurt by the time it came to rest.

They climbed down the tree onto the snow-packed ground. To their relief, the temperature was an unseasonably balmy 30°. However, there was no sign of human life. The aeronauts realized they were completely on their own. Since the Navy didn't know where they were, no one would be able to rescue them. They had to rescue themselves.

They had no supplies and no water. But they did have matches and their three caged pigeons. The men set off at a fast clip, heading toward the south-east in hopes of finding the barking dog—and, hopefully, civilization. They traveled until dusk and then built a fire of rotten wood and pine brush for the night. Silently, the three downed balloonists stared into the crackling flames, wondering what fate awaited them.

Hearing what he thought was a stream, Hinton decided to look for it. They desperately needed water. After trudging through the dense forest for a while, Hinton became overheated, so he took off his heavy flight suit and laid it on the ground. He continued his search for fresh water but the woods closed in on him. Soon he didn't know where he was or where he had left his flight suit. He started walking faster and faster but it all seemed to be taking him down the wrong path.

Finally he noticed the smell of burning pine and followed his nose back to his companions. Through the night the men huddled together for warmth. Kloor's feet were so close to the fire that his boots were singed.

After a fitful sleep the shivering men killed one of their pigeons, roasted it, and ate it for a meager breakfast. For water they resorted to dipping into "moose licks," small holes made when moose lap up snow.

They set out Wednesday morning, weak from lack of food and drink. On they trudged, heading east, toward the sound of the barking dog, which they heard from time to time. They finally reached a creek and drank their fill. They decided to follow the creek downstream, but soon a fierce winter storm blew in, bringing heavy ice and snow and plunging temperatures. The men could walk for only about two hours before their feet became so cold that they had to stop and build a fire. In fits and starts, they pressed on until nightfall.

After a dinner of caribou moss, the men made camp along the banks of the creek. The storm had stopped but the temperature had plunged below zero. Except for the crackling of the fire, the rustling of the trees, and the occasional howl of a wolf, it was oddly silent.

"Where do you suppose we are?" Kloor asked.

"Somewhere in New York," offered Hinton.

"Nah, I say Canada, the woods," Farrell said. "Think we'll ever find that dog?"

No one answered. For a long time, they fell into a glum silence, staring into the flames.

"Something will turn up tomorrow," Hinton said. "I know it. It'll be the third day."

They all nodded their heads, as if Hinton had just uttered some great words of wisdom. As hope faded and superstition took hold, the men were clinging to the old seaman's belief that the third day of a journey will bring good luck. "Something will turn up," Hinton repeated.

Trial by Balloon

Kloor and Farrell dozed off while Hinton stayed up for several hours watching the fire. They slept in shifts to make sure that the flames didn't die out. Still, none of the men managed to get much shut-eye, and that deepened their misery.

The third morning, Thursday, brought them nothing that felt like good luck, just hunger, weakness, and nausea. Worst of all was the uncertainty. They had no idea whether they were one mile or one hundred miles from the nearest human. Because they had kept the compass, they knew for sure that they had not been walking in circles. But that was small consolation.

"I think we should write farewell letters to our loved ones and put them in our pockets," Farrell suggested. "That way, if they ever find us, they'll know our last thoughts were of them."

"There'll be plenty of time for that later—if we ever give up," Kloor replied.

For breakfast they killed and ate one of their two remaining pigeons. The men decided it would be bad luck to kill the third pigeon. Besides, the little birds yielded no more than two ounces of meat per man, not much to travel on. They set the surviving bird free because they didn't want to continue toting its cage. Everything was becoming unbearably heavy. Through the day as they walked, more slowly and painfully with each passing hour, it became clear that the pigeon cage was the least of their problems.

Farrell had started to lag behind, and Hinton suggested it might be wise for him to ditch the heavy flight suit, which he did. Under his flight suit Farrell had only his long underwear, and he continued the trek in nothing but that garb. Walking was so strenuous that it kept him from freezing. Hinton had of course lost his suit and Kloor had cast off his heavy suit earlier in the journey; both were traveling in only thin shirts and jackets. The cold was hard to endure, but the suits were just too heavy to wear.

At one point, Farrell stumbled over a log, fell headlong, and slashed his shins. Helping Farrell up, Hinton heard the flier murmur words he couldn't quite believe he was hearing. "I'm not going to make it," Farrell muttered. "Cut my throat, take my body for food. Let me die."

"Don't talk like that," said Hinton. "You're just fatigued. We have to stick together, and if that time comes, then we'll die together."

"We have to keep moving," Kloor said. "We're getting closer to the dog."

After staggering along the creek bank, they came to a clearing and finally found the barking dog that had fueled their belief a house was near. But instead of shelter they found irony. They had come upon a stray husky caught by the leg in a beaver trap—and it was sending out its own call for help. They freed the dog.

Despite their hopeful superstitions, their third day in the frigid wilderness was ending in much the same way as the previous days—with hunger, agony, and the looming realization they might not get out alive.

On the fourth day, they reached a frozen river and discovered that they could make much better time walking on the ice than through the snow along the bank. But making better time to where? They decided to head east.

While they slowly trudged through the bitter cold, Kloor spotted something that revived their spirits: sled tracks.

The three desperate aeronauts quickened their pace and soon covered about five miles, until the tracks came to a frozen lake about two miles wide. Then they saw a heartening sight. Off in the distance, about a mile ahead of them, they could barely make out the form of a man. Mustering all their strength, they shouted, hooted, waved, leaped, and tossed their arms above their heads, hoping to catch the eye of the stranger.

They finally succeeded. The man, a local Cree Indian trapper named Tom Marks, took one look at the tattered trio—especially Farrell in his torn, baggy long underwear—and their frenzied dance, and then he did what he thought was the only sensible thing to do. He bolted, thinking that he was seeing spirits.

They shouted in English and French for him to come back. Although he knew only a few words of those languages, something in their tone made him believe they were in trouble and not dangerous. He turned and warily walked toward them. Through hand signs, grunts, and the offer of cigarettes, Kloor managed to convey their desperate situation. The Indian gestured for them to follow him. Kloor took a few steps, then turned to discover that neither of his companions was behind him.

"I can't go on," Farrell groaned, as he tried to stand. "I just can't."

"I'm played out too," muttered Hinton.

They were so close to rescue, yet they couldn't move. Reluctantly Kloor went on alone to follow the Indian and promised help would return.

For two hours Kloor and the Indian trudged through snow and ice. Finally, to Kloor's elation and relief, they arrived at a cluster of rustic cabins with smoke curling from the chimneys. It was a small settlement of white and Indian fur traders who spoke English.

"Are we in New York?" Kloor asked his hosts.

"No, Canada," one of the trappers grunted. "This is the settlement of Moose Factory."

It was an old, remote Hudson Bay trading post in

Trial by Balloon

the wild northwestern region of Ontario. The winds had carried the balloon 1,200 miles from its base to an area just south of James Bay. The fliers were about 600 miles off course.

The luck that seemed to desert the three men when the wind pushed them so far into Canada could actually have been worse. Had the wind taken them a little farther northeast, they would have been carried over Hudson Bay and would likely have come down in an even more desolate, deadly area.

Soon a rescue party was dispatched to retrieve Farrell and Hinton, and now the famished Kloor devoured plates of bacon and moose meat. Soon his fellow balloonists, ragged and starving, staggered through the door and sat down to eat their first real meal in nearly a week.

With their bellies full and their bodies in warm clothes, they penned quick messages to their loved ones. Kloor told his fiancée that the experience had been like "passing through the tortures of hell." He also wrote a note to the Naval Air Station that they were safe. A messenger at Moose Factory then left to deliver the messages to the nearest telegraph office in Mattice, Ontario, 200 miles away.

Meanwhile, the men stayed at Moose Factory for ten days, building up their strength and writing more and longer letters to their relatives. Their letters were taken to Mattice by Indian runners who wound up suffering frost-bitten faces in the ever-worsening weather. When the outside world heard of their ordeal, it was inevitable that the press would eagerly pursue their story. More than a dozen reporters headed to meet them in Mattice.

Back in Moose Factory, the aeronauts celebrated Christmas with the traders who made them presents of bags of candy, a tiny British flag, and a Canadian pin. Three days later, the trio had regained their strength and were ready for the next part of their journey—mushing out of the wilderness via the Missinaibi Trail to Mattice, where they would get on a train for the trip home.

But if they thought their worries were over, they were wrong.

They were severely tested again when they and their three guides left the trading post on dog sleds. By now the snow was four feet deep and the temperatures had plunged to 40° below zero. On the treacherous Missinaibi Trail, they slogged through blinding whiteouts and stinging blasts of wind-whipped ice particles while three teams of eight sturdy huskies pulled the supply sleds. Three times, the fury of a blizzard forced the men to bury themselves in snow caves and wait out the storm.

Despite being clad in thick fur, they battled the horrible tortures of deadly cold that searched for any exposed flesh. With each breath the super frigid air seared their lungs. Adding to their misery, the balloonists suffered "snowshoe sickness," a condition that painfully attacks the nerves of the legs. It's caused by lifting the weight of the snow-caked snowshoes mile after mile. It tormented Hinton so badly that the only way he could walk was to tie a piece of rope to the back of each snowshoe and lift it at each step with his hands.

During the arduous walk, the aeronauts uncharacteristically bickered with each other over the slightest irritation, their tempers triggered by the hardships and grueling struggles that they had to endure. But as quickly as the quarrels flashed they subsided.

The trail was unbroken almost the whole way, so the men had to go ahead and tamp it down as hard as they could. Legs burning and feet blistered, the weakening trio had to keep up a steady pace with their guides or be left behind. For 14 grueling, punishing days, they trekked in the bleak, barren snowscape, until finally on January 11 they reached Mattice.

Incredibly, within 15 minutes of their arrival, a bitter argument erupted between Hinton and Farrell. Ignoring their friendship, which had grown stronger through the escapes from death they had shared, Farrell launched into an obscenity-laced tirade against Hinton in front of shocked newspaper reporters who had traveled to Mattice to interview the survivors. Then Farrell struck Hinton in the jaw, knocking him over a table before reporters could restrain him. Farrell's fury had been ignited by a reporter's revelation that Hinton had written letters claiming Farrell was the weakling of the group. The letters had been published in the press. Further agitating Farrell was his belief that Hinton had violated an agreement that the three of them had made back in Moose Factory to sell their story to the highest bidder. (Yes, even back then survivors were savvy about checkbook journalism.)

A few hours later Farrell and Hinton, who was sporting a shiner, patched up their differences and Kloor issued a statement claiming the fight was "a passing flare-up attributable to overwrought minds and overwrought bodies."

The following day they boarded a train for New York, where they were greeted by hundreds of well-wishers who released tiny balloons in tribute to the aeronauts' survival.

Kloor told the public that the secret of the trio's survival was their collective strength. "We have sacrificed for each other mutually and without partiality and have fought the battle out as one composite group of shipmates. In accordance with the best traditions of the great United States Navy, we did all we could to uphold our own dignity, and will forever be brothers and the best of friends."

THE FROZEN STOWAWAY

Like most young boys, Armando Socarras Ramirez had many dreams for his future, dreams of winning baseball games, taking pretty girls to dances, going to high school and becoming a painter. Most of all, Armando dreamed of freedom, but that was off limits for a boy like him. He was a young man living in the 1960s in Communist Cuba, a country where freedom was a dirty word, a word that could be uttered only in hushed tones in private places, if at all.

Armando could not quiet the voice in his head that kept saying, "Escape, Armando. Escape." It was the first thought when he woke up. It tortured him throughout the day. And it was the last thing he thought about before he dropped off to sleep in his home in Havana, a miserable one-room flat crammed with 11 members of his family. He thought about freedom while he was playing baseball, his passion, and he dreamed of it while strolling with his sweetie, beautiful Maria Esther.

When Armando reached the age of 16, he became desperate. That year, even those simple pleasures—his ball games, his girl—were ripped from him when the government whisked him off to the village of Betancourt miles from home. There at a trade school, Armando was promised that he would receive training to become a welder. But he didn't learn much because he and the other boys were often yanked out of the classroom to toil in the sugar-cane fields.

Armando did as he was told, but secretly he thought of nothing but getting away. His uncle had escaped to America. Now Armando wanted to follow him, no matter what it took, no matter what he had to leave behind. The teen could not stand being told what to do all the time, what to think, where to go, and where he couldn't go. Even breathing made him feel guilty. Every time he took a breath, he imagined Fidel Castro looking over his shoulder, scowling.

Armando looked with envy on other Cubans, the lucky ones who were allowed to take one suitcase on an airplane and leave, never to return. He held out little hope that he'd ever be sitting in one of the two planes of passengers whom Castro allowed to leave the country each day. There was a waiting list of more than 800,000 desperate to get out.

The Frozen Stowaway

He was afraid that even by asking to be put on the list he would be viewed by authorities as a *gusano*, a worm, and they would take away what little he had in property and respect. It got to the point where he believed that if he didn't at least try to escape he wouldn't be able to look at himself in the mirror every day.

When he was 18 and had returned from Betancourt to Havana, Armando made a new friend, Jorge Perez Blanco, 16. At first, they talked about their love of baseball. Then, in whispers they revealed their other passion: freedom.

Jorge, though, had gone a step beyond daydreaming. He had figured out a way to escape. Once a week there was a flight from Havana to Madrid, Jorge told his new friend. The flight was always booked solid months in advance. Somehow Jorge and Armando would sneak onto that plane. They didn't know how far away Madrid was, but they didn't care. From then on, the two made a study of the planes leaving for Madrid, looking for any opening that might let two small, slender boys slip on board as stowaways.

It came to them one day as they lay on the grass outside the airport fence looking at the sky, watching an Iberia Airlines DC-8 pass directly overhead, its wheels still down. "There's enough room in there for us," Armando said to Jorge, as both peered up into the wheel well. Armando was only five feet tall, and 120 pounds; his friend Jorge was even smaller.

They came up with a plan that they were sure would work. It just *had* to work.

They knew that departing airliners at Havana's Jose Marti Airport taxied to the end of the runway, turned around, stopped momentarily, and then took off. The two young men planned to rush up to the plane during its brief stop and hop into the wheel well. They would bring rope to tie themselves inside and stick cotton in their ears to protect against the shrieking noise of the jet engines.

On June 3, 1969, Armando and Jorge arrived at the airport about an hour before the scheduled 6:30 P.M. departure of the Madrid flight. Sweating and shaking—more in fear of being caught than of the danger they were about to face—they huddled behind the fence at the end of the runway, waiting for the red and silver jet to taxi near them before takeoff.

When the pilot turned the plane around and waited for clearance to take off, Armando kicked his companion, who was trembling so hard he could barely move. "Come on, let's go!" Armando yelled. They dashed to the plane, and Armando climbed up onto one of the massive 42-inch-high wheels and grabbed a strut. He pulled himself into the small wheel well on the right side. Jorge headed for the wheel well on the left.

The Frozen Stowaway

With a jerk and a roar, Iberia Airlines Flight 904 barreled down the runway at 170 miles per hour, carrying 10 crew members, 147 passengers, and two stowaways. Holding tight to pipes along the side of the tiny compartment, Armando looked down and saw a big wheel, still hot from takeoff, slowly retracting toward him. Terrified that it would crush him, he kicked at it with all his might, but it continued to move toward him as he squeezed against the roof of the well.

He sucked in his breath to gain a couple of inches and then closed his eyes in case it wasn't enough. If he had miscalculated, he didn't want to see his own death approaching. But with about four inches to spare, the wheel locked into position and the wheel-well doors closed. In total darkness, Armando waited, wedged into a tiny space between the wheel and the roof of the compartment, clutching the conduit and wires on either side. It was too confining for him to move his arms, so he couldn't tie himself to the conduit.

"Jorge! Jorge!" Armando shouted. "Are you okay?" But Armando couldn't hear a response above the din from the wind and jet engines.

Meanwhile, in the cockpit, Captain Valentin Vara Del Rey noticed a blinking warning light indicating that the wheels had not properly retracted. He radioed Havana. "There is an indication that the right wheel hasn't closed properly," the 44-year-old pilot reported to the control tower. "I'll repeat the procedure."

Just as Armando settled into what could pass for a comfortable position, he was stunned to see the wheel-well doors open again. He had no idea what was happening, so he grabbed a pipe and held on for dear life with dreadful thoughts swirling through his mind. *What if someone saw me? What if the plane is turning around?* He imagined that even now Castro's police were at the end of the runway, waiting to haul him and Jorge off to prison.

Soon, however, his fears were eased as the wheels folded up again and locked into position. The door closed once more, again leaving him in darkness. He had made it! Armando started to relax.

But now he faced a new danger. As the plane climbed, the compartment grew colder. At that moment, Armando, who was wearing just a thin shirt and pants and one shoe (the other had fallen off when he jumped onto the wheel), realized that he had overlooked an important fact.

He hadn't considered that the wheel well wasn't airtight, wasn't pressurized, and wasn't heated. He didn't know that the plane was climbing to 29,000 feet, about the height of Mt. Everest, where oxygen and warmth are in short supply. Nor did he know the air up there is so thin that humans without proper gear aren't expected to survive.

The Frozen Stowaway

As the plane soared over the Atlantic, temperatures in the wheel well plunged to 40° below zero. Armando's thoughts drifted to the people he had left behind—especially his parents, five siblings, and girlfriend—before he grew drowsy and fell into a strange, deep sleep.

Nine hours and 5,563 miles later, the plane landed at Barajas Airport in Madrid. When the plane arrived at the gate, Armando—unconscious, nearly frozen, and curled up in the fetal position—tumbled out of the wheel well and onto the concrete tarmac at the feet of mechanics who had begun servicing the craft. His lips were blue, his skin was ghostly white, and his body was covered with a thin layer of ice. When a momentarily stunned member of the ground crew realized that a body had fallen out of the wheel well, he rushed over and felt Armando's heart. "He's alive! He's alive!" the man shouted.

"That's impossible! Impossible!" declared Captain Vara Del Rey. "No one in a wheel well could have survived this flight." But miraculously Armando had survived.

Quickly, the airport workers wrapped the frozen boy in blankets and gave him oxygen before rushing him to Madrid's Gran Hospital de la Beneficencia. When he arrived at the emergency room, his body temperature was so low doctors couldn't even get a reading on a thermometer.

When he regained consciousness several hours later, one of the first things Armando noticed was how doctors kept staring at him and shaking their heads.

"Am I in Spain?" he asked when he opened his eyes.

"Yes," replied Dr. Jose Parjares. "Madrid."

Tears welled up in his eyes. "They're not going to send me back to Cuba, are they?"

Dr. Parjares shook his head. "You're safe here."

"Where's Jorge? He was with me."

No one in Spain knew the answer. But Cuban authorities did. Sadly, Jorge had fallen from the wheel well as the plane was taking off, and he died almost immediately.

Meanwhile, Spain's top medical experts were amazed that Armando had survived the thin air and brutally cold temperatures, especially because the slim young man was wearing light clothes appropriate to the Caribbean climate. Yet somehow here he was, alive, asking questions while thawing out his frozen fingers in a bowl of warm water.

No one could say for sure, but doctors speculated that Armando's heart actually had stopped beating sometime during the trip. "Very few human hearts, if any, have endured what your heart has endured," Dr. Parjares told Armando. "Your ordeal is astonishing, one of the most remarkable feats of endurance in medical history."

The Frozen Stowaway

The scientific explanation was that the extreme conditions had pushed his body into a "superhuman fatigue," a state akin to hibernation. The temperatures around him dropped slowly, gradually reducing his need for oxygen. When he thought he fell asleep, he had really passed out because he couldn't breathe.

Airspace was crowded that day over Madrid, which also turned out to be a lifesaver for Armando. The pilot had to circle, and he descended slowly, allowing the young man's frigid body to start a gentle thaw, as if he were coming out of hibernation.

Another bit of good fortune was that he had hitched a ride in a plane with a skilled pilot at the controls who made an exceptionally smooth landing that day. A hard landing might have jostled the unconscious young man's frozen body out of his hiding spot and to his death on the runway.

When Armando recovered, he eventually flew to the United States—this time inside a plane as a passenger—where he enjoyed a tearful reunion with his uncle, Elo Fernandez, who had escaped from Cuba two years earlier and now lived in Passaic, New Jersey. Armando went to live with his uncle, attended school, and studied to become an artist.

Shortly after his arrival in America, Armando told a local reporter, "I often think of Jorge. We both knew the risk we were taking and knew that we might die in our attempt to find freedom. But death seemed to us better than living under the repression of Cuba.

"I suppose it was lucky that one of us made it. And knowing the risks and what happened to my friend, I would try it again if I had to. Life without freedom is a life that is worthless."

ADRIFT IN PURGATORY

Even amid the grim daily dispatches of savage battles and dead GIs during the first year of World War II, Americans were particularly upset when they heard the news on October 22, 1942: A B-17 Flying Fortress on a secret mission for the War Department had disappeared somewhere over the vast Pacific. Among the missing was 52-year-old Eddie Rickenbacker, the country's ace of aces during the previous war.

The idea that he might be dead was something Americans simply could not accept—the dashing, fearless flyboy seemed, like the country itself, to be indestructible. The "Darling of Lady Luck," people called the tall, square-jawed, handsome hero.

Time after time he had slithered out of the grasp of death's bony fingers, beginning when he was a race-car driver who survived more than a dozen serious crashes. In World War I, his legend grew when he took on seven German planes at one time; he shot down two of them and sent the others fleeing. Showing those Germans what Americans were made of, Rickenbacker downed a record 22 enemy planes and four combat balloons, which earned him the Congressional Medal of Honor.

After the war, Rickenbacker became head of Eastern Air Lines and established a glowing safety record for his company. But on February 27, 1941, he escaped another brush with death when an Eastern plane he was in crashed near Atlanta, killing eight passengers. Despite being pinned under the wreckage and critically injured, he directed the rescue of the surviving passengers before he himself was freed hours later. After four months in the hospital, he returned to his job. "I'm a hard man to kill," Rickenbacker boasted.

So when word came that Rickenbacker's B-17 had vanished in a particularly treacherous part of the Pacific, the same immense stretch of ocean that five years earlier had claimed the life of the famed aviatrix Amelia Earhart, people at first refused to believe it. They held on to the hope, however slim, that their hero would be found. One of the biggest search and rescue efforts ever was launched, but as the days turned into weeks, it seemed that Rickenbacker's luck had run out.

Adrift in Purgatory

Rickenbacker's latest saga began on October 21, 1942, just 20 months after he nearly died in the Eastern crash, when he stepped aboard a B-17 in Honolulu, Hawaii. He was on a secret mission to an island near New Guinea to give classified information to General Douglas MacArthur, commander of the Allied Forces in the Pacific.

Sporting a fedora and walking stick and accompanied by his friend and aide, Colonel Hans Adamson of the U.S. Army, Rickenbacker introduced himself to the awestruck crew members: Captain Bill Cherry, pilot; Lieutenant James C. Whittaker, copilot; Lieutenant John deAngelis, navigator; Staff Sergeant James W. Reynolds, radio operator; and Private John Bartek, engineer. Also on board was a passenger, Sergeant Alex Kaczmarczyk, a soldier rejoining his regiment in the South Pacific after recovering in a Honolulu hospital from a serious bout of jaundice. Other than Adamson and the 41-year-old Whittaker, the other men had been in diapers when Rickenbacker was shooting down planes above the Western Front.

The doomed flight of the B-17 began ominously when a wheel inexplicably locked on takeoff, sending the plane careening toward a hangar. Cherry averted a deadly disaster when he deliberately spun the craft in several ground loops before stopping.

After switching to another B-17, the eight men

took off again at 1:29 A.M. and climbed to 10,000 feet above a thick cloud cover. Later that morning, about 1,700 miles southwest of Hawaii, the plane glided down under the clouds to 1,000 feet, but the men saw no sign of land. Only then did they discover that they had strayed off course because an important navigational instrument, a portable octant, had been jarred slightly out of whack during the earlier aborted takeoff. The pilot had followed the flight path based on the erroneous coordinates of the octant.

"We're lost," Cherry announced matter-of-factly.

The plane had enough fuel for another four hours. The pilot radioed the island's airfield for assistance in getting a fix on their position, but the airfield didn't have the necessary equipment to help determine the plane's position. Cherry then asked the airfield to fire some anti-aircraft shells timed to explode at 8,000 feet as a signal. After the plane climbed back up to 10,000 feet, Rickenbacker and the others onboard peered out the windows looking for black bursts that would help them locate the island. But the men saw nothing but empty sky.

They had two choices: They could continue to fly blindly in the slim hope of finding a friendly base before their fuel ran out or they could ditch the plane in a controlled but dangerous water landing. They decided on the latter option. The timing had to be perfect because the plane needed to land parallel to the waves in a trough. If the craft hit the crest of a wave, it would break apart as thought it had smashed into the ground. Ditching was risky—up to that time no B-17 had ever been put down at sea without loss of a life.

The men prepared for the maneuver by lightening the load to soften the impact. They tossed luggage, mail sacks, and personal items (including Rickenbacker's new Burberry coat), a suitcase that had been a Christmas gift from his Eastern employees, and a briefcase bulging with important one-of-a-kind documents. Rickenbacker even pitched his spare dental bridge out the hatch. However, Whittaker kept a pencil and a diary, which he always had with him, and Bartek held on to his khaki-covered Bible.

Before throwing his suitcases overboard, Rickenbacker retrieved a handful of handkerchiefs that he thought might help protect them from the sun. The men filled thermoses with coffee and water and piled emergency rations just below the hatch from which they planned to escape. They sent out a "Mayday" call and then prepared to crash in the ocean.

The pilot and copilot pressed seat cushions against their bellies, pulled their safety belts tight, and started a long dive. As they got close to the water, Bartek ripped open the escape hatch. From then on, all they could hear was the deafening roar of wind as they sped at about 100 miles per hour toward the water.

Rickenbacker had positioned himself in the radio room, where he watched through a small porthole as the plane headed closer to the water.

"Give us the score, Captain!" one of the men yelled.

"We're now at five hundred feet," Rickenbacker called back. "Four hundred, three hundred . . . about a hundred feet to go." A few more seconds passed as the plane continued to head toward the water. "Only fifty feet left! Hang on to your hats! Here she comes!"

When they were about one foot above the surface, Cherry pulled back on the wheel with all his might, forcing the plane's nose up so that the tail would smack the water first. From 90 miles an hour, the plane came to an abrupt stop in a violent jumble of shattered steel and glass that flew around the crew's heads. Rickenbacker had heard such a horrible sound on only one other occasion: the Eastern crash that nearly killed him.

Thanks to Cherry's skill, the plane landed perfectly. Everyone was alive and not seriously hurt except for cuts and bruises although Adamson had badly wrenched his back. As water rushed in through the broken windows, all eight men scrambled out onto the wings and inflated the plane's three small emergency rubber rafts. Rickenbacker, Adamson, and Bartek were in one raft; Cherry, Whittaker, and Reynolds in a second; and deAngelis and Kaczmarczyk in a smaller one called a Donut. The men in the larger rafts were so cramped that they had to lie with their arms around each other and the two in the Donut had to sit face-to-face with their legs looped over the other's shoulders.

"Who has the water?" someone shouted out.

There was no answer.

"The food?" the same voice called out. Still there was silence.

In the confusion following the landing, no one had grabbed the food supplies. The men looked around, hoping to find something, but there was nothing. For a moment they considered going back into the plane for the supplies, then decided against it because of the fear of being caught when the plane plunged to the bottom. Six minutes after the plane ditched, the tail turned up and the Flying Fortress disappeared beneath the waves. It was shortly after 4:30 P.M. October 22, 1942, the first day of their voyage through a watery purgatory.

The ocean, which from a few thousand feet above looked as smooth as bathtub water, heaved in rolling swells 8 to 10 feet high. For the first several minutes, the men could do nothing more than vomit into the sea from shock and motion sickness. Kaczmarczyk continued retching long after everyone else's stomachs had calmed down.

Meanwhile, the eight men studied their predicament. They were crammed into three tiny yellow rafts stranded in the middle of who-knows-where in the South Pacific. They had flares, aluminum oars, lifejackets, and fishhooks. To eat they had just four small oranges that Cherry had stuffed into his pocket. They had no water. Sharks menacingly circled the pathetic little flotilla.

The men knew their chances of being found before they died of thirst or hunger were slim at best. But they refused to think about that. They had to keep hoping and finding ways to stay alive. So they strung their rafts together, hoisted a sail fashioned from an undershirt, and rode the waves like a roller coaster. The swells sprayed them, coating their skin with salt that stung their cuts.

That night they set off a few flares, but there was no response.

The next day, Rickenbacker tried to fire up the crew. "We'll be picked up today for sure. I'll give a hundred dollars to the first man to spot the plane or ship that rescues us," he announced, encouraging them to scan the skies as diligently as they could. But no ships appeared on the horizon; no planes in the sky.

Following Rickenbacker's advice, the men covered

Adrift in Purgatory

their heads, fashioning hats from their undershirts and his handkerchiefs. The sun's piercing rays baked them most every day. Two men with darker skin tanned quickly, but the others, including Rickenbacker, blistered and were soon covered with red, oozy burns down to the soles of their feet. A few tried to escape the burning rays by paddling in the water, but it only made matters worse later on after they climbed back into the rafts and felt the sting of the sea salt as they dried off in the breeze.

They slept in shifts with at least one man on the lookout at all times for rescuers. Rickenbacker dozed no more than an hour a night because he was worried the lookout would drift off to sleep and miss a chance for them to be rescued. But there was nothing to see, just rolling waves and wispy clouds. Days into their ordeal, Rickenbacker began seeing the clouds turn into shapes of elephants, trees, and even beautiful women. He thought he was hallucinating until he confided in Adamson, who revealed that he too was seeing images in the sky.

As hot as it was during the day, it was chilly at night. When the stars came out, Rickenbacker often asked Adamson, who once had been in charge of the New York Planetarium, to keep the men's minds off their discomfort by giving lectures on the constellations.

By cutting each orange into eight slices and eating

one slice a day, the men made their only food and liquid last for four days. That was hardly a meal and a drink. Their hunger pangs grew so strong that the men considered desperate measures like slicing off their fingertips, toes, and earlobes to use for bait. They bandied about the possibilities and asked Rickenbacker his opinion. "Flesh would serve as bait if it should become necessary," he tersely commented, and said no more about the matter. They drifted on.

On the fifth day, the starving men could think of nothing but food. They talked about steaks, roasts, and turkey, and heaping platters of mashed potatoes. They became so obsessed with food that Cherry pretended to have a pad and paper and began taking orders for dinner.

Bartek pulled out his soggy New Testament and, in a soft whisper, started reciting scripture from Matthew 6:31–34: "Therefore, take no thought, saying, what shall we eat? Or, what shall we drink? Or wherewithal shall we be clothed? . . . For your heavenly father knoweth that ye have need of all these things." The words provided solace to the men, a possibility that they would survive. Still, without food or water, it was hard to keep faith.

But later that day miraculously, a small bird, probably a sea swallow, fluttered down from the empty sky and perched right on Rickenbacker's head while he was dozing. He quickly awoke but remained still before cautiously reaching up and grabbing the bird. Cherry killed it by wringing its neck. The meager meal of raw, stringy bird meat hardly satisfied their hunger. But the bird's intestines were used as bait to catch a few good-sized fish. Although raw and somewhat disgusting, the fish provided nourishment. Later a school of minnows swam by and ended up being scooped into the boat and swallowed whole, three minnows to each man.

The next day, another bird landed on Rickenbacker's old felt fedora, which his wife had been trying to get him to toss out for about 10 years. He caught the second bird, but for some reason didn't have the heart to kill it. "Do we really need to kill this one?" he asked. "We still have plenty of bait to fish with." So, in an incredible act of faith, floating in the middle of the ocean and with no guarantee of future meals, he let the bird flutter away.

But even worse than the hunger was the unbearable thirst. The body can go a few weeks without food but only a few days without water. Their parched throats yearned for water, and the men battled against the urge to take a drink from the ocean. They could think of little else but their craving for life-sustaining, refreshing water.

Each day, the men pulled their three tethered rafts close together for a daily prayer service. Later, the men, each in his own way, started having conversations with the Almighty, even if they hadn't been particularly religious before.

"See what you can do for us, Old Master," said Cherry one evening after setting off a flare. It was a dud, but it caught fire anyway before falling back into the water. Lured by the sputtering light of the flare, two fish came close enough for the men to snare them. Rickenbacker then cut the fish into equal morsels and doled them out.

As the sun rose to its brutal, scorching height on the seventh day, Adamson was in great pain from his back injury and grew increasingly morose. He was so despondent that he slumped over the side and into the water. Rickenbacker quickly snatched him back from the sea and then cursed him out using words as blistering as the sun.

"In my condition, I can't do anything," Adamson lamented. "I thought it would be better if I were out of the way, so there would be more room and food for everybody else—and a better chance for your survival."

"We will have no quitters in these boats!" Rickenbacker barked. "And no one will do anything stupid or selfish to lower the morale of the others. Understood?" Although he was looking at his aide when he spoke, he was directing his remarks to all the men.

Adrift in Purgatory

The veteran military man, drawing on his experience in more than one tough scrape, knew that his men were beginning to give up, the first step toward certain death. They began to bicker and complain. His only hope was to shake them up by verbally abusing them. So he lashed out at the men in language that even rough-and-tumble military men weren't comfortable repeating.

It worked.

"Rickenbacker, you are the meanest, most cantankerous son of a bitch who ever lived!" one man shouted out after a particularly rough session. A couple of them vowed to live, if just for the pleasure of burying the old bully at sea.

Once during their odyssey, Rickenbacker overheard one of the men praying to God to take him. "Cut that out!" Rickenbacker bellowed. "Don't bother Him with that whining. He answers men's prayers, not that stuff."

In fear of another tongue-lashing from the living legend, they all struggled to keep their spirits up, even as their own tongues were swelling from lack of water and the sun was burning the skin off their backs and faces.

On the eighth day, they recited the Lord's Prayer. No sooner had the sound of the last "Amen" drifted off into the salty air than Whittaker noticed some clouds drifting by. First they were small, white and fluffy, but soon they darkened and clumped into a huge bluish-gray mass. It could only mean one thing. Rain!

A cloudburst exploded right over their rafts, showering them in torrents of heavy drops. In rapturous disbelief, they turned their eyes to the heavens and felt the cool water bathing their skin. They cupped their hands and guided the life-saving raindrops into their parched throats for the first drink they'd had in a week.

They looked for a way to store fresh water. All they had for reservoirs were the insides of their inflatable Mae Wests. But these life vests had extremely small valve openings. So the men sopped up the rainwater with T-shirts, wrung out the water into their mouths and then spit it into the tiny valves of their life vests.

To the men's glee, the refreshing storm lasted for an hour. But then, to their dismay, a gust overturned their rafts, sending all but one of the waterlogged life vests to the bottom of the sea. They were now left with only a quart of water.

The water and the prayer services kept them going, and each day they invented new ways to stay alive, even as new problems, such as painful saltwater ulcers on their arms and legs, kept appearing.

On the eleventh day, another rain squall buoyed their spirits until a wind tipped one of the rafts over and dumped Kaczmarczyk into the water. When he was pulled back into the tiny two-man Donut, it became clear to everyone that he was very sick. Kaczmarczyk was still frail from his recent two-month hospitalization for jaundice and was not up to an ordeal that would test the bodies and souls of the most hale and hearty of men.

Thirst, hunger, exposure, and exhaustion sapped what little strength and willpower he had left. His condition was made worse because he had made the deadly mistake of drinking seawater. He became delirious and didn't recognize anyone. Rickenbacker moved him into the larger raft and held him in his arms to protect him from the spray and keep him warm during the night. Kaczmarczyk rallied the next day, but then, while mumbling endearments to his mother and girlfriend, he died during the night. At dawn of the thirteenth day, the seven survivors said a prayer and slipped the young soldier's body overboard. They watched his body slowly float away, leaving them more depressed than at any previous time since they had ditched.

From then on, they struggled to keep their hopes up even as fate seemed to be turning against them. Their spirits sank, the salt ulcers on their legs deepened, and the few wisps of clothing that shielded them from the sizzling rays had started to disintegrate. Hunger had so weakened them that the slightest effort was exhausting. They hadn't eaten in days because their fishing line had rotted in the salt air.

On the fourteenth day, their little rafts slipped into the doldrums, where there was no wind, no current. For the next four days, they barely moved on water as smooth as a sheet, leaving the men with nothing to do but scream delirious curses at the sun. Their water supply was as low as their hopes.

During this time Rickenbacker worked hardest to keep the men motivated. He lashed out at anyone who uttered discouraging remarks, blasting the offender with a barrage of expletive-laced putdowns.

In the late afternoon of the eighteenth day, their spirits suddenly soared when they heard the muted roar of an engine. About three miles away in the sky they could make out a seaplane. With no flares left, they roused their painful, weakened bodies and made a feeble attempt at shouting and waving. But the pilot didn't see them.

The crushed men sunk into a silent, devastating gloom. But then Rickenbacker let loose with another verbal assault, accusing them of being weak-willed babies. "If we saw one plane there has to be more of them," he argued. "If the rafts are close to a base, then they'll get closer tomorrow and the day after. Good things are coming—and only real men will have the courage, the patience, and the faith to wait for them."

Over the next two days the men saw a patrol plane pass nearby, but its pilot failed to spot them. Again, a little bit of the will to live drained out of the men, and again they would be verbally savaged by Rickenbacker's sharp tongue. Their only moment of joy during this miserable time was when a brief shower quenched their thirst and gave them reason to hope.

Finally, Cherry, now alone in the Donut, took a desperate gamble. He cut his raft loose. "If we all spread out over a wider area, we'll have a three-to-one better chance of being seen," he explained. The others agreed and cut the line between the other two rafts, Rickenbacker, Adamson, and Bartek in one and Whittaker, Reynolds, and deAngelis in the other. The men said goodbye, and by nightfall of the twentieth day the three rafts had drifted so far apart that they could no longer see each other.

The gamble paid off.

The next morning, Cherry was roused from sleep by the sound of a Navy plane heading straight toward him. He jumped up in his tiny Donut and frantically waved. To his unbridled jubilation, the seaplane landed next to him.

"Who are you?" the seaplane pilot asked.

"I'm Captain William Cherry, United States Army

Corps. And you are the greatest sight I've seen in weeks!"

Although exhausted beyond belief, Cherry excitedly told the pilot that the other survivors had to be nearby. The Navy then launched a huge search and rescue operation in the general area of the Phoenix Islands, 600 miles from Somoa.

Meanwhile, earlier that morning, Whittaker had been shaken awake by deAngelis. "Hey, what's the matter with you?" Whittaker snapped.

"Jim," replied his raft mate, "I think you'd better take a look. It may be a mirage, but I think I see something."

It was no mirage. In the distance, about 10 miles away, they could see dozens of palm trees! His two crewmen were too frail to paddle, and so Whittaker paddled against a current for nearly eight agonizing hours, until they reached the beach of a remote island and collapsed on the sand, their first solid ground in three weeks. They were soon discovered by friendly islanders who tended to them. The following day the fliers were spotted by Navy search planes after Cherry told rescuers where to look.

It was now the twenty-fourth day. Buoyed by the rescue of four of the survivors, the Navy scoured the ocean for the one raft, still bobbing alone. Meanwhile, the lengthy ordeal had taken its toll on its three occupants. Their eyes sunken and their withered bodies pocked with ulcers, the feeble men languished in their raft, wondering if they would ever get rescued. And then . . .

"Eddie," whispered Bartek, "I hear a plane!"

With barely enough strength to lift his head, Rickenbacker weakly waved his arms at two Navy patrol planes directly overhead. The aircraft circled them and rocked their wings, letting the castaways know they had been seen.

Hours later, a Navy seaplane landed next to the raft. There wasn't enough room in the small plane for all of them, so Adamson, who with his injured back was in the worst shape, was squeezed into the cockpit. Rickenbacker and Bartek were lashed to the wings, and the plane taxied on the rolling sea for 40 miles to land, where the men were taken to a Marine hospital for treatment.

Back in the United States, headlines screamed, RICKENBACKER DOES IT AGAIN; RESCUED WITH 5.

The front-page news fired up the fighting spirit of America. Even the comic-book crimebuster Dick Tracy was inspired. In one strip, Tracy trudges through a blizzard with a dying infant in his arms. Soon exhausted, Tracy falls into the deep snow, ready to die. Then his hands reach down and touch the edge of an old newspaper buried in the snow. When he pulls it out, he sees headline DYING OF

HUNGER, RICKENBACKER AND CREW PRAY. *If Rickenbacker could do it,* Tracy thinks, *I can do it too.* The feeling was shared by most Americans.

Before returning to the United States, Rickenbacker, his eyes swollen and hands bandaged, told of his faith during the long vigil. "I am not formally a religious man, but I can truthfully say I never doubted for one moment that we'd be saved. . . . I hold to the Golden Rule, and I believe most firmly that if a man just follows what he truly knows and feels in his heart, then he can't go wrong and is possessed of religion enough to get by in any man's land."

Later, back in America, he admitted to reporters, "I know I came within hearing distancc of the Old Fellow this trip, because the approach is always the same, is unmistakable. One hears beautiful music, and everything is extremely pleasant—just as heaven should be."

"So," one reporter challenged, "you're sure you are going to heaven?"

Rickenbacker, who would not learn what the Almighty had in store for him for another 30 years, smiled and said, "Say, I guess that was presumptuous of me at that."

THE OMEN

He was young, handsome, and British born, but that's not what set the staff at Montreal's ritzy St. James Hotel abuzz about Mr. Samuel Hilditch, the brainy 25-year-old partner in the drug company of Messrs. Evans, Mercer & Co.

What triggered the flow of gossip was a bizarre conversation he had with the front-desk clerk at the luxury five-story hotel on the morning of March 17, 1873. "Where might I inquire about finding lodging in a small house with a family?" he asked. Beads of sweat were forming on his forehead and his eyes were as wide as those of a frightened deer.

Alarmed by Hilditch's strange demeanor, the clerk gave him a recommendation and then asked, "Is there a problem with your accommodations at this hotel?"

"No, no," Hilditch said nervously, trying to pretend everything was fine when clearly it wasn't.

Then he leaned over the counter and whispered, "Don't you see the smoke? There's going to be a fire!" His lip quivering and brows furrowing, he hissed, "I will not stay another week in this hotel. Something bad is going to happen!"

He was right. Something bad did happen later that night at the St. James.

Johanna O'Connor, a petite, 20-year-old who worked as one of the hotel's kitchen maids and lived in a room on the fifth floor, wasn't all that surprised when word reached her about Hilditch's foreboding premonition. She assumed his fear of a hotel fire sprang from the heavy smoke that had been billowing from the St. James's kitchen-laundry annex for several days, the result of a faulty flue. Workers had tinkered with the flue and claimed that the problem had been fixed.

Johanna was about to leave the kitchen and go up to her room when the hotel's night watchman and bookkeeper showed up. "Mind if we take a look at the stove?" the watchman asked. "Some guests are complaining of smelling smoke." The men peered into the large wood-burning stove for a few minutes. "Looks all right to me," the watchman said, and the bookkeeper nodded in agreement.

They turned to leave but Johanna stopped them. "I have a funny feeling about it," she said. "I told the workmen I think something's amiss. I told them yesterday but they said it was nothing to worry about. I still think something's amiss."

The two men looked at each other, then peered into the stove again, but they could find nothing wrong. So they tipped their hats, bid Johanna good-night and left. Johanna stared at the stove and shook her head. *It's that Mr. Hilditch filling my head with rubbish,* she told herself. Then she went to her top-floor room, which she shared with another hotel maid, and quickly fell asleep.

Shortly after one A.M. on March 18, Johanna was jarred awake by the sounds of screams, running feet, and banging. "Girls! Girls! Get up! The hotel is on fire!" the night watchman yelled.

Smoke slithered into her nostrils, triggering a coughing spasm. While the sleepy Johanna tried to gather her senses, her roommate shouted, "Get out now! There's not a second to spare!" Wearing nothing but her nightgown, her roommate bolted out the door.

Still in a fog, Johanna tried to follow, but she didn't get far. Smoke had filled the corridor until it was so thick she couldn't see. Gasping for air, she jumped back into the room, slamming the door behind her. She hurriedly tossed on some clothes and decided to brave the hall again. By now the smoke had become even denser. With her hand over her mouth, Johanna groped in the deadly darkness for the stairwell but she was lost in the maze of hallways. Choking with every step, she stumbled blindly through the thick, black smoke.

Meanwhile, amid shrieks and great commotion, the St. James's guests were fleeing the flames, which were quickly consuming the hotel. Many were rushing out of the building to safety while others were standing by their open windows, pleading for help. Some patrons were flinging their belongings, hastily stuffed into suitcases and steamer trunks, through their room windows. Others, unwilling to wait for help, had ripped the sheets off their bed and knotted them together and were using them to lower themselves to the street. But in many cases their makeshift lifelines were too short, leaving the people dangling helplessly 20 to 30 feet in the air before the horse-drawn fire wagons arrived at the scene.

Back on the fifth floor, Johanna assumed she was the only person left in the smoky corridor. She was frantically working her hands over the walls trying to find a stairway to help her escape. With breathing now almost impossible, Johanna soon crumbled in a heap of despair to await her death, when suddenly she heard a man's distressed voice through the acrid blackness. "Where are the stairs?" he asked loudly. "Where are they?"

Johanna leaped to her feet and followed the sound of the voice while flailing her arms in all directions.

The Omen

She soon felt a man's coat and held on tight to the back of it. "Help me find a way out!" she wailed.

"I can't see a thing!" The man gasped between smoke-induced coughs. "Do you have match?"

The question seemed ludicrous to Johanna—*He wants a match when we're trapped in a fire?*—but these last few minutes seemed incredible to her too. *I can't believe this is really happening to me. I'm going to die.*

The man kept moving forward and Johanna kept clinging to him. Unwilling to breathe in any more smoke, she held her breath until her lungs felt like bursting.

"What's this?" the man said. He turned a doorknob and the two tumbled into a gas-lit room and closed the door. Johanna caught her first glimpse of the man and recognized him as Mr. Thomas, a boarder who worked at the nearby Ontario Bank. They turned around and saw Mr. Hilditch, paralyzed in cold terror, cowering in the shadows next to the window.

"Open the window!" Thomas ordered.

"I can't," Hilditch whined. "The window is stuck!"

Thomas picked up a chair and hurled it through the glass. The three of them rushed to the opening and gulped in deep breaths of fresh winter air. Then they leaned out and screamed for help.

Seeing flames leap from the windows in the stories below her and realizing the ladders were far too short to reach the fifth floor, Johanna slumped against the wall and closed her eyes. The merciless smoke was curling up from under the door and filling the room. *We're doomed,* she told herself. *It's only a matter of time.*

Their darkening little refuge turned stifling hot until, in a flash, fire burst into the room. Seconds later, with a great whoosh, the bed went up in flames.

"I will not die by fire!" vowed Hilditch, his eyes wild with panic. Then he let out a plaintive roar, ran to the window and dove out headfirst.

Down below, Fire Captain William Orme McRobie was rushing into the building when he heard a dull thud. He didn't even turn around, assuming it was just another steamer trunk full of clothes that someone had tossed out. But then Assistant Fire Captain Richard Choules cried out, "Oh, for God's sake, Captain, come here quickly!"

McRobie spun around to confront a sickening sight. Sprawled on the pavement was Hilditch's broken body bleeding from sharp crisscrossed gashes made when he fell through the telegraph wires.

Five stories above in Hilditch's now superheated room, Johanna shouted to the firemen below, "Don't let us burn to death!" Her thin, light voice cut through the frigid morning air. "Help us!"

By now the deadly flames had unrelentingly advanced to within two feet of the window. Johanna and Thomas knew they had run out of all options—except one.

"Come on!" Thomas urged as he began to climb out the window. "It's the only way!"

Unlike Hilditch, Thomas didn't jump. Instead, he held on to the windowsill and slowly lowered himself, his fingers clinging to the indentations in the brick wall, until his foot felt the top of the protruding two-inch-wide frame of a fourth-floor window. But that was as far as he could get because smoke and flames were spewing out of the room beneath him. With all his might he kept his fingers pressed hard against the cold wall and hollered for help.

From below he heard encouraging words from concerned onlookers who were watching the drama unfold from Victoria Square: "Don't let go!" "The ladder's coming!" "Hold on!"

Glancing down from the corner of his eye, Thomas saw firemen lean a ladder against the building, but it was much too short to reach him. Thomas struggled to hold on, but one after another, his fingers slipped off the brick. A few excruciating seconds later, he lost his grip. Helplessly plunging to what he thought was certain death, Thomas passed out.

"Noooo!" wailed Johanna as she leaned out the fifth-floor window and watched him fall.

The flames now had engulfed the room and

singed her hair. When her dress began to smolder, she knew she had no choice. Gingerly, she stepped out onto the windowsill and grasped the top of the window frame with her right hand. She hung on, screaming for help, as the crowd below gasped and begged her to hold on.

Meanwhile, two firemen, John Beckingham and John Nolan, were manning the department's longest ladder, which reached only to the third story. Beckingham had scrambled about two thirds of the way up the ladder when he realized that the young woman would be way beyond his reach. He yelled down to Nolan, who dashed to the fire wagon and returned seconds later with another, shorter ladder.

Nolan passed the short ladder up to Beckingham, who lifted it toward Johanna. It came several inches short of the windowsill. "Step on the ladder and climb down," he ordered her. "I'll hold the ladder."

With trepidation she tried to step on it, but as she put her weight on it, the ladder dipped dangerously; Beckingham couldn't hold it steady from his angle. She remained on the windowsill as Beckingham pulled the ladder back.

Holding the second ladder, he climbed the taller ladder until he was balanced precariously on the topmost rung. Carefully he turned around and pressed his back against the wall. Then, with near superhuman strength, he raised the second ladder above him until Johanna was able to grasp it with her left hand. It was cold and slippery, coated with ice from water that had frozen in the frigid air.

"C'mon, Miss, grab it," Beckingham implored her in a voice trying to sound calm.

"I can't," she whimpered as stomach-turning thoughts clouded her brain. *I'm going to die. If I try to climb down this ladder, how can he possibly hold on? What if I slip or lose my grip? One false step and it's all over—and I'll probably take him with me. This is pure madness!*

With Beckingham sandwiched between the wall and the second ladder, Nolan climbed up the tall ladder until he was directly beneath Beckingham. Then he hollered up to Johanna, "Don't be afraid. Just take your time and come down slowly."

The petrified Johanna glanced down at the firemen and nodded. Her hands were cold, clammy, and numb even though flames were flickering out the window. She closed her eyes and murmured to herself, "Courage, Johanna. Courage." Then ever so slowly she took the ladder with both hands and moved her body out until her feet touched a lower rung. The ladder dipped under her weight, causing her to whimper.

"That's it, Miss. Very good," Nolan said. "Slowly now, steady."

His arm and leg muscles burning and shaking

from the strain, Beckingham gritted his teeth and maintained a death grip on the ladder.

Johanna lowered her body onto the wobbly ladder. She could hardly breath. Her head started spinning and she thought for sure that she was going to faint. "Courage, Johanna. Courage." She took a deep breath and continued down, one icy rung at a time, cautiously placing each foot before daring to lift the other.

"Slowly, good, that's it, that's it," Nolan said encouragingly.

Sweat trickling down his face, Beckingham could barely tolerate the agony in his pain-racked, trembling limbs. He was so consumed by his determination to hold the ladder that he couldn't utter a word, only piercing grunts.

In a tense minute that seemed to take forever, Joanna descended past the fourth-story window, then past Beckingham and into the waiting arms of Nolan, who was braced near the top of the tall ladder. As soon as she felt him hold her, Johanna burst into tears of relief. He cradled her in his arms and carried her to the ground, where they were surrounded by a wildly cheering crowd.

Looking up at the inferno, Johanna lamented, "I have lost everything."

"Everything but your life," Nolan said.

"You're right," she replied, snapping out of her

feelings of self-pity. "I can never thank you firemen enough for saving my life."

"Yeah, but you showed plenty of courage standing out on the window ledge for twenty minutes and then climbing down that ladder. Not many people could have done that."

Suffering from cuts and burns, Johanna was taken to the hospital, where to her happy amazement she learned that Thomas was alive and would survive. After he had lost his grip, he fell two stories and struck the ladder that Nolan and Beckingham had set against the wall to save Johanna. Thomas bounced off the ladder and landed on a fireman, who cushioned his fall.

Dozens of people were injured that night in the fire which was caused by a faulty flue. Three people died, including Hilditch, whose terrible premonition of a deadly fire turned out to be all too true.